CURSE
OF THE
WITCH ILONA

An eerie crawling traced up Brak's naked spine. The witch Ilona pointed to the heavens. Already tendrils of the ebony stormcloud were whipping above the ship's frayed pennons. Ilona's lips moved, but her words lost meaning. Brak continued to stare, fascinated. Ilona swayed. Her body went rigid. Tears of hate, of defeat, streamed on her cheeks. For one awful instant her luminous eyes focused on Brak, on Brak alone of all those who were her enemy. She made his face a part of her memory of the defeat she had suffered.

Also by John Jakes

BRAK THE BARBARIAN (Tower 51650)
BRAK VS. THE MARK OF THE DEMONS
(Tower 51651)
BRAK VS. THE SORCERESS (Tower 51709)

JOHN JAKES

BRAK:

When the Idols Walked

TOWER BOOKS NEW YORK CITY

A TOWER BOOK

Published by

Tower Publications, Inc.
Two Park Avenue
New York, N.Y. 10016

Illustrations by Ron Miller

Author's preface

About a week ago, one of the guests at my daughter's wedding reception asked me a question I didn't expect. "What's happened to Brak?"

I was taken aback, but pleasantly so. So much attention has focused on the Kent Family Chronicles in the past few years that sometimes I almost forget that an earlier series of mine (and one of my favorites) attracted an audience no less loyal than that of the Kents.

Hence my pleasure when I heard the question. The audience is still there, it seems.

The gentleman who asked the question holds a doctorate in psychology—another nice proof of the wide appeal of fantasy literature in general, and sword and sorcery in particular. When I was reading fantasy works in my teens, it was assumed that only slightly daffy kids were interested in that kind of writing. Today only the uninformed offer such opinions.

It was in the role of dedicated Conan fan that I wrote the first Brak tale, *Devils in the Walls*. In spirit, anyway, the story was a Howard pastiche, and I have acknowledged the fact more than once. Still, as literary characters often do, Brak soon took on a distinctive life of his own. Sometimes the changes in his personality, story to story and book to book, surprised even me.

I put together this first collection of Brak tales in the late 1960's. Since its initial publication in 1968, it has never been out of print; well, not for more than a few weeks, anyway. I'm pleased that this Tower edition will maintain the continuity.

With a little luck, one of these days I may find time to add some new pieces to the canon. I hope the gentleman who asked the question would enjoy that. I know I would.

John Jakes

October 10, 1980

From the storm-lashed Dark Sea the scaly headed apparition loomed over the manacled rowers in the war galleys. In the air, strange powers battled, and demons walked the waves. Striding tall amidst the terror: Brak the Barbarian, who here begins another adventure of sword and sorcery.

Chapter I

DOWN FROM THE NORTH ROLLED thick black stormclouds. They swept the sky like an enemy in pursuit, spreading from horizon to horizon. The wind increased. The mighty sails of the war galleys beating along the Dark Sea snapped and cracked. Blazoned upon the great blood-hued sail of the admiral's flagship was a gigantic, crudely-painted image of the horned goat-god of the Gords. The god's leering face seemed to grimace in awful contortions as the wind rose still higher, tearing at the sail.

In the rowing pits of the flagship, bedraggled men turned their heads to watch the ominous clouds boiling in the wake of the armada. Many of the rowers bore scabrous wounds on their bodies. All were ill-clad. Most had the sick shine of defeat in their eyes. Above the moan of the wind and the crashing of the Dark Sea's waters against the flagship prow, a faint muttering of fear broke out.

Wrists and ankle-chains clanked. More of the rowers turned to stare behind them at the darkness closing down upon the Gord fleet.

One of the men chained in the pits smiled a cruel smile as he craned his head around to stare at the blackness. He was a man who did not seem to belong in the chains that held him fast to the oar. His body was gigantic, wide-shouldered. His arms were brawny. His yellow hair was twisted into a long, barbaric braid that hung down his back. His only garment was a lion's hide wrapped around his middle.

From the quarterdeck of the flagship the row-master's gavel began to hammer faster.

"Stroke! Stroke! Stroke!"

The yellow-haired man stared with sullen pleasure at the clouds boiling up close behind the fleet of seventy Gord warships. He muttered, "These pig-soldiers who attack their neighbors without warning or provocation deserve to be swallowed up in such a foul sea. I'd welcome the sinking of the whole lot of them, though I don't especially want to go with them. But there's no chance of outrunning that cloud. It blows too fast, too blackly."

The rower next to the big man did not care to comment. He merely whispered, "Turn around, barbarian! Else we'll— ah, the gods protect us! Why was I unlucky enough to be chained next to a savage?"

"You!" came a shout from the walkway between the pits. "Barbarian! Pull your oar!"

Slowly the great-shouldered man whose name was Brak looked up. On the walkway stood the Gord overseer fingering his coiled lash. Brak's eyes burned in the lead-colored light that covered the Dark Sea from cliff to coastal cliff. Resting on his oar, Brak spat.

The overseer's arm went back, snapped forward. The long lash coiled around the barbarian's chest.

When it tore loose it left a serpentine of blood around his torso. Brak came to his feet in the swaying pit, growling angrily, yanking at his chains.

The prisoner beside Brak was gibbering, begging him to

be calm. But the pain of the whip had inflamed the barbarian. For a moment he was without reason. He pulled wildly on the chains and made growling sounds, like one of the beasts of the wild lands of the north from whence he had come.

A huge wave broke across the bow of the Gord flagship. Spray cascaded over Brak. The cloud of hate passed from his mind.

Another wave struck amidships. The galley rolled. Brak tumbled onto his bench with his leg-chain tangled. The overseer laughed. He drew the end of his whip through his free hand to wipe away the blood, walked on.

But the overseer's assertion of power was of small consequence. The war-fleet was rapidly being overhauled by the storm. The pitching of the flagship became more erratic. Smaller ships fell behind.

"Stroke!" cried the rowing-master from the quarterdeck. "Stroke! *Stroke!*"

Brak fell into the rhythm, hauling on the oar with the six other men on the bench. He felt a dismal gloom, created not so much by fear of the impending storm as by his helplessness against the threat posed by his captors' fright. When the whirlwind from the black clouds struck, they would soon enough forget their cruelty to the hundreds of prisoners who, like Brak, were helping to row the Gord soldiers homeward. But in their forgetting, in their panic, the ships might be destroyed. Brak had no illusions about the Gords wishing to save their slave rowers.

The big barbarian felt naked without the broadsword that had slapped against his hip only two days ago. That day, his pony's hooves had carried him down from a plateau to the little port city of the Mirkan people, at the head of the Dark Sea.

Bound on a long journey to seek his fortune in the warm climes of Khurdisan far southward, Brak's arrival in the city of the Mirkans was wholly accidental, the result of a chance turning in the road. Arriving, he had gone to sleep on a pallet in a flea-bitten caravanseri. He intended to rise next dawn and continue his journey.

During the night there had been drumming. Men with torches shrieked alarms in the streets. The Gords, short, squat men who wore leather armor trimmed with fur, had appeared out of the night to attack the Mirkans. At the same time, the Gord fleet engaged the pitifully few fighting ships of the Mirkans off the harbor mole.

The day's fighting had been a holocaust. On his huge body Brak still bore cuts and small scars. He remembered lopping off several heads in the caravanseri yard while the sky reddened with flames of the sacked town. But the Gords had the double advantage of surprise and numbers. Like most of the able-bodied Mirkans, Brak had been caught.

He was herded down to the Gord galleys and impressed as a slave-rower. Only the sudden appearance of the stormclouds in the wake of the triumphantly homeward-bound Gords had lessened the success of the attack in which Brak had been trapped by accident.

"Stroke!" cried the rowingmaster. *"Stroke!"*

Brak bent his huge back into the effort. Silently he raged against the poor fool calling for greater effort. It was obvious that the ships, even with a combination of sail and oars, could not outrun the storm. The black clouds were closer now. They covered the northern horizon from sea to heaven.

The soldiers on the flagship gripped their spears and leather-clad shields and watched, helpless, while the Gord admiral, a porcine, bearded stump of a man, exhorted the rowingmaster to quicken the beat still further.

Slightly ahead and to port of the flagship, Brak noticed a jutting headland. As he pulled mindlessly on his oar, he saw several of the Mirkan captives give sick smiles, whisper among themselves. Gradually, as the war-fleet drew abreast of the headland, Brak could make out a large, up-thrusting island. It separated a huge bay into two channels. Through blowing mist the buildings of a great city were barely visible on the coast behind these bays. Inside a tall watchtower on the headland, torches flickered like weird little fire-flies.

"Well," said the Mirkan who earlier had urged Brak to curb his temper, "there's one kingdom these sons of hell won't live to destroy. Quite a joke, isn't it?" The man's scrawny ribs thrust against his emaciated chest in a spasm of weak laughter. "To save Rodar's people we shall all have to be drowned, together, friend and enemy alike."

"Who is Rodar?" Brak asked. "The ruler of that place partly hidden in the mist?"

"Aye. The city-state is under the dominion of Rodar, Prince of the Two Bays. It's been foretold that the Gords want to be masters of the whole of the Dark Sea. They began with us, the Mirkans, at the northern end. Certainly Rodar's kingdom would have been next. Though small, it's the most powerful on the entire sea. Rodar himself has always known the Gords for what they are—beasts, whose only purpose is conquest. While the Mirkans have always dwelled far enough away from the Gords—so we thought—to remain free of the contest, all who live along the Dark Sea long ago realized that, one day, the Gords would strike at Rodar. His kingdom has prided itself on decency and justice, while the Gords—"

Before the glass-eyed Mirkan could finish, a cheer from the soldiers burst raggedly through the noise of wind and sea. Brak and the other prisoners glanced up.

On the quarterdeck, the Gord admiral no longer wore an expression of fright. He was smiling, bowing forward a young woman who had emerged from the cabin in the stern's castle.

"That's the strangest sight of any yet," Brak said, his thick yellow brows pulling together. "A young girl on a warship."

The Mirkan alongside shuddered. "Not an ordinary girl, outlander. Her name—"

But the Gord soldiers were already chanting it:

"Ilona! Ilona! Ilona!"

They beat their spear-heads against their leathern shields. Brak recalled hearing frightened Mirkan men whisper the name in the burning streets. The young girl negotiated the tilting deck with ease. She moved to the rail. A peacock-hued cloak belled out from her shoulders. Beneath this a pearl-colored gown was pressed tight against her body by the wind. Her hair was yellow, like Brak's. Her face was comely, oval, red-lipped, the brows delicate. Her eyes were large and luminous as sapphires.

The girl lifted her pale white hands in a kind of benediction. The gesture seemed to quiet the soldiers, and lend the admiral confidence. But the Mirkan slaves in the pits quickly averted their heads.

"Many people said a woman called Ilona was with the Gords when they attacked," Brak whispered. "Who is she?"

"Their witch. Their sorceress. Don't look at her."

Despite the warning, Brak continued to study Ilona. To all outward appearances she was as fresh and attractive as a country bride. Yet the tiny smile on her mouth, the glow in her eyes as she stood with upraised hands, hinted otherwise.

An eerie crawling traced up Brak's naked spine. The witch Ilona pointed to the heavens, above the rattling, cracking sail. Already tendrils of the ebony stormcloud were whipping above the ship's frayed pennons. Ilona's lips moved, mumbling something. An incantation against the elements?

Brak continued to stare, fascinated. Ilona swayed. Her body went rigid. The Gord admiral watched the sky—

Abruptly, the tendrils of cloud that were sweeping down upon the seventy helter-skelter ships of the war-fleet began to curl back upon themselves, parting, ripping away to vapor, as though the storm had been stopped by a magical power.

The Gord soldiers began to beat their shields again. They cheered their good fortune.

Suddenly, from another of the galleys foundering along nearby, a sea-trumpet bleated. Then again. Its notes were like the wail of a frightened soul.

Ilona dropped her arms to her sides. She took a step backward. The admiral clutched the rail. One of the Mirkans two benches forward let out a cheer. The admiral seized a soldier's spear and, cursing, flung it out, hard. The Mirkan took the spear in his belly. He pitched over backward with blood spilling from his middle and washing down his death-thrashing legs.

"In the name of the unseeable," Brak said, "what madness is on them?"

"Madness?" The voice of the prisoner beside him quaked. "Not madness, barbarian. Fear of revenge!"

Whipping his head around, Brak saw what the admiral, Ilona and the soldiers had sighted first.

A low, fast warship with a prow carved in the shape of a gryphon's head had come darting out of the total blackness of the stormcloud covering sea and sky in the north. From the ship's prow swayed a great cross-barred lantern radiating bluish light. Above the lantern, somehow managing to stand upright on the swaying figurehead, was a man, little more than a blur of gray robe and white beard.

Already the strange new ship, being much lighter, had passed several of the Gord galleys. It bore down upon the flagship.

"Kalkanoth!" sobbed the man beside Brak. "That is his sacred lantern, and there he stands! At least if we must die, then he will make certain many a Gord dies with us."

Once more Brak was puzzled. "Who is it?" he shouted above the storm. "Some Mirkan general?"

"Our warlock! Kalkanoth, our sorcerer! He's old and wise

enough in the magical arts to humble Ilona and this pack of butchers. Had Kalkanoth been in our city when the Gords struck, we would have had some chance to win. But he has been many months in the inland wilderness, alone, on a pilgrimage.''

Now the Mirkan seemed almost hysterical with joy as he went on, "Clearly one of our people lived long enough to locate him, and guide him back. He has come, through the storm, on his own ship, to take revenge—"

Brak was not impressed. What was the arrival of the warlock but more futility? One tiny craft, one ancient wizard against seventy vessels, a young witch and a mammoth storm to boot? Brak shook his head as the flagship began to pitch violently again.

Hardly a rower moved now, nor a Gord overseer either. All were watching the strange new ship with its great lantern spreading bluish light ahead of it.

Powerful or not, Kalkanoth could do no more than destroy himself along with the Gords. That was hardly reassuring to Brak. The nightmare of the storm and the hopeless odds against the revenge-crazed warlock of the Mirkans could only result in a holocaust of death. A holocaust which would sweep Brak the barbarian—in chains—along with it.

Somehow, Kalkanoth remained standing on the fig- urehead as his craft drew within two lengths of the Gord flagship. The smaller vessel cut a path through foundering enemy ships. Here and there bowmen or spear-bearers threw their weapons at the speeding little gryphon-vessel, but the casts fell short.

Again Brak cursed. That he should be caught in this orgy of self-destruction, of hate-induced madness—it sickened him. What a pitiful spectacle it was! Kalkanoth was no more than a blur in the blowing storm-mist. His tattered gray robe flapped, his beard flew as he made meaningless, intricate patterns in the air with his old white hands.

*   *   *

Ilona stepped forward to grasp hold of the quarterdeck rail with her left hand. Her right hand was raised again, fashioned into a claw. She motioned with it, as though trying to draw something out of the blackening sky. Suddenly, down from the apex of the heavens where the ebony clouds were closing in, a clap of thunder boomed.

The roar made Brak's head ache. His ears throbbed. Gord soldiers screamed. In the instant of their terrified crying, the whole sea lit up with the blaze of a bright scarlet streak of lightning.

Like a sword it smote down out of the darkness. The lightningbolt struck the sea, burst into a ball of fire and steam.

Two benches ahead, a Mirkan was on his feet, foaming at the mouth, beating his fists against his oar.

"Kalkanoth will avenge us! Kalkanoth brings the dark powers!"

The Gord admiral hastily consulted with Ilona. He seized a bronze trumpet, shouted through it: "Have no fear! Ilona knows the secret ways of our enemy. His tricks are illusion. The storm makes it easy for him to conjure up spirit-demons. The celestial ether is disturbed, full of strange impulses. Ilona will banish his phantoms—"

Hysterical screaming from a nearby Gord vessel drowned him out. Brak gaped.

A wash of scarlet light suddenly came bubbling up out of the sea. And in the crown of light that covered the churning waves between the flagship and Kalkanoth's vessel, two great baleful eyes in a gigantic scaled head appeared—

Then a dripping, slimy body high as a galley's rail and twice as long. The apparition rose from the Dark Sea with ten lashing forks in its tail and immense webbed fore- and hindclaws. Towering far above the flagship, it seemed to claw its way along the water without touching the surface.

Another crackling streak of red lightning split the sky.

Another. Another. With each burst a new, incredible *thing* took shape out of the sea—

Here reared a wing-shaped monster with one staring eye in its round head; there, a creature materialized that was no more than a writhing mass of sucking tentacles twice as long as the highest Gord mast. Like evil flowers the creatures bloomed from the sea's surface on every hand. Brak bit his lip until he tasted blood.

On the flagship quarterdeck, Ilona's claw-shaped hands convulsed, opening. The tips of her fingers spit little hissing lines of white radiance. But her face was a mask of rage and despair.

In the oar-pits, the Mirkan prisoners began to tear savagely at their chains. Gord soldiers ran for the rail, moaning in terror. Vainly the admiral cried through his trumpet:

"Be calm! They are mind-phantoms! Ilona knows—she will dispel them!"

Ilona tore the trumpet from his hands, cupped it to her mouth. Her voice was a thin wail as she vainly tried to restore order to the scene:

"I cannot fight alone! I cannot dispel them unless the power of your minds will aid me. Believe they're phantoms! They are, they are! You must believe it! Your thoughts must cry out that Kalkanoth's demons are false, that they will vanish before your eyes if—"

Ilona's words cut off abruptly as a contingent of Gord seamen from the quarterdeck rushed past her, knocking her against the rail. One after another, the seamen leaped overboard. They preferred watery death to the approach of the lizard-like head, all red-shiny, that was craning down upon the flagship from above.

Brak's mind could not calmly absorb so much horror, so many unthinkable ten-armed, five-headed, tentacled things. One moment they seemed insubstantial as fog. He could see through them. Then they would solidify again.

Waves broke higher over the flagship, higher still. The air around Brak was turning to scarlet mist. Ship after ship, foundering without rowers, was going down. Afar off now, Kalkanoth's blue lantern still burned.

In the oar-pits more screaming broke out when the baleful eyes of the lizard-thing dipped down between the masts. Oarsmen threw themselves into hideous convulsions to escape the all-too-real phantoms with which Kalkanoth was gaining his revenge. The oar to which Brak was chained snapped in half. One end lashed around, impaled the Mirkan who had been fettered next to him. The splintered shaft pierced the man's chest, emerged from his back.

The big barbarian was on his feet in a tangle of bodies and blood. He pulled frantically at his own chains when he realized that his wrist-links were broken away from the shattered oar. Beneath his feet the deck planks were cracking apart as the flagship rolled dangerously.

Brak scrambled over the tangle of foam-lipped prisoners. He charged for the rail. A hand gripped his naked shoulder. Brak whirled.

A Gord overseer, mindless with fear and the urge to strike back, lifted his short-sword to cleave Brak's skull.

The barbarian crouched, snapped his right hand forward. The broken end of his wrist chain struck the overseer between the eyes, shattered flesh and bone. The man dropped, his eyesockets erupting with gore.

Instinctively Brak reached out, caught the man's short-sword. As his fingers closed on the haft, there was sanity in him again. For with a weapon, small as it was, he felt less helpless.

As he started for the rail, a misty red claw, six times as wide as a man, coiled over the rail's edge from below. The claw was real and yet not real. Brak turned. He preferred to try another route of escape, rather than plunge through part of the body of the monster whose great head waved above the snapping masts.

The big barbarian scrambled over rioting, mindless men who tore at one another, friend and foe alike. At last he gained the quarterdeck. There he saw an open bit of rail again. Beyond lay the sea, where a hundred horror-creatures writhed among wrecked ships.

He plunged ahead, yellow braid streaming out behind him. A squat, round-eyed thing that had been a man stumbled into his path. The admiral.

Brak dodged aside. The admiral mewed and moaned, dimly recognized a tangible enemy. He drew back his spear to drive it through Brak's belly.

The barbarian jumped aside. But not fast enough. The spear-head ripped his thigh, drawing blood.

Brak thrust out with his right arm. The short-sword gutted the admiral through the bowels. As the dead man fell away, Brak froze.

Clinging to the lashing wheel was the witch Ilona.

Tears of hate, of defeat streamed on her cheeks. For one awful instant her luminous eyes focused on Brak, on Brak alone out of all those who were the enemy.

Her garments were soaked. She looked old and bent despite her youth. But for that long moment, she looked upon the face of Brak the barbarian, who had slain a Gord admiral, and she made his face a part of her memory of the defeat she had suffered.

Her lips jerked. Her hand lifted, palsied, as though she meant to curse him. Brak stared, shuddering. The instant was long as eternity—

Before Ilona could cry out, a wave thundered over the quarterdeck. The force of the wave knocked Brak through the air, splintering wood, carrying Ilona away, whirling the world in confusion.

He struck the sea with cruel force. He twisted over and over, fought his way to the surface. His thigh throbbed. His chest burned. He felt pitifully weak. The admiral's spear had gouged too deeply.

All around, men and wreckage drifted. The men were as shattered as the remains of the ships.

All around, the great vessels of the Gord fleet sank. The monsters of Kalkanoth faded away to mist. Of the warlock's gryphon-vessel there was no sign.

But the damage was done. The Gord fleet was destroyed. As Brak swam, he heard the rush and roar of the flagship going down behind him.

Even the sky was growing lighter. Brak saw the coastline a great distance off.

But the waves were high. His arms ached as he pulled himself through the water.

He knew he would not make the shore.

Then he knew nothing at all.

Chapter II

SWIRLS OF ORANGE LIGHT BEAT against Brak's eyelids.

He was conscious of a slow, pulsing pain in his leg. The pain numbed his whole body.

He fought to open his eyes. His hands closed into angry fists, tangling in a wine-colored woolen coverlet upon which he lay. The lion-hide garment was still wrapped about his middle. Otherwise there was no familiar reference point. It was as though he had emerged from a pit of total forgetfulness into a place of sulphurous light; a place where a grotesque, elongated shadow convulsed on a tapestried wall, bending toward him like some gate-keeper of the Underworld—

"The shore," Brak croaked, dizzy. "The shore is too far. I remember—"

He stopped, gaping. He remembered it all, including the lashing of the waves, and his conviction that he was fated to die in the Dark Sea. All at once, the scene around him sharpened.

It was no misty entrance-chamber to Hell. The mist was all in his eyes, and clearing. The sulphurous glare was the flicker of an oil lamp on a pearl-inlaid taboret. The shadow on the wall of the commodious bedchamber was a trick of lamplight. The shadow belonged to a slender, gentle-faced young woman with auburn hair down to her waist. The girl wore a spotless white gown and was bending over Brak.

"Can you hear me at last, stranger?"

"Aye."

"For nearly a month I've watched, waiting for you to come back to your senses."

"A month?" Brak scratched his head. "Who are you? What is this place?"

The girl smiled, though not without a trace of apprehension. Probably this was the result of his appearance, Brak guessed. Half-naked, the big barbarian all but hid the pallet on which he lay, so huge was his frame. There was clean linen bound around his thigh where—he remembered it—the Gord admiral's spear had dug deeply.

"I am Saria," the girl said. "Perhaps my father and Calix should explain the rest."

As the girl moved gracefully toward the doorway hangings, Brak sat up. He grimaced. Pain stabbed down his leg again.

"Is your father one of the Gord people, girl?"

Ugly and tense in the lamplight, Brak's face frightened her, stilled the reply on her lips. She merely shook her head. Then she was gone in a rustle of hanging silks.

Brak scowled. He stood a bit unsteadily. He stretched, glanced around the large, airy chamber.

A high window embrasure revealed a patch of stardusted sky. Through the window drifted street noises, the creak of a wheeled cart. The sounds were vaguely comforting. Had the battle on the Dark Sea been an evil dream?

Brak knew it had not. He bore the wound in his flesh as a

token of that ghastly encounter. He bore the memory of the sorceress Ilona's eyes remembering his face.

Voices murmured on the far side of the hangings. Quickly the curtains were swept aside. Into the chamber strode a man of middle years and medium height. He was clad in a costly green robe whose hem was stitched in gold thread, in a repeated pattern of the balance-scales of the market place. The man wore a short beard, grayshot. His general appearance was kindly.

Behind, in the simple gray tunic of a freedman, came a second man. He was younger, with curly red hair, startlingly bright blue eyes and well-muscled arms. In contrast to the swarthy looks of the older man in the emerald robe, the freedman's coloring was light. Circassian, Brak guessed.

The bearded man paused a safe distance from Brak. "I am Phonicios. This is my house."

"My name is Brak. I gather I owe you a debt. But what sort of debt still puzzles me."

Phonicios studied him. "We are equally puzzled. You are not a Mirkan. Neither are you one of the Gords. Yet we found you—rather, my steward Calix discovered you—" A small ruby on Phonicios's right hand glittered as he indicated the freedman. "—lying on the shingle of the Dark Sea, unconscious, the night after the great battle of the ships. That was almost a month ago. Since then you have dreamed and raved endlessly. Many times we thought you would die. We had the devil's own time feeding you by force, I might add."

"How did you happen to come upon me on the coast, steward?" Brak asked.

Calix smiled easily. "My master had sent me on a mission. My first impulse was to leave you where you lay. But the chains on your wrists and ankles convinced me you hadn't been aboard the Gord ships out of choice. So I loaded you into the chariot and brought you here, for Lord

Phonicios to deal with. Lucky for you that the chief of the Merchant Guild has a tender-hearted daughter.''

Here Calix glanced warmly at the girl Saria. She returned his gaze for an instant with equal warmth, then glanced away, flushing. Calix went on, wryly:

"I'd not have sat with you all this time, stranger. As far as I'm concerned, you have the look of trouble about you."

Phonicios frowned. "Don't judge him thus simply because he's an outlander, Calix. Mind your tongue."

Reassured that he was among friendly people, Brak managed a smile. "An outlander I am indeed, lord Phonicios. My name is Brak. More often than not, strangers call me a barbarian because, in the high steppes where I was born, our dress and manners are not so elegant as here in these civilized lands. I was a prisoner on the Gord flagship, and—but before I tell that tale, I have one question. Where is this house? I mean, in what city?"

Pulling up a stool, Phonicios poured wine from a silver amphora and gestured for Brak to drink.

"This is the city-state ruled by Rodar, Prince of the Two Bays." Phonicios scowled. "Would the Prince were here to protect us, instead of that bumbling vizier who will lead us like lambs into the jaws of the Gords before he's done."

"Rodar," Brak murmured, brows together. "I recall now. We saw the city from shipboard."

"And our lookouts," put in Saria, "saw the conflict on the sea from the coastal watch-tower. Awful red fires—frightful creatures rising from the waves." The girl's slender yet womanly figure shuddered lightly. "The tales of it terrified the city."

"As well they might," Brak said low. "I have seen demons aplenty in my time. But never any so large as those conjured up in the battle between the witch and the old man on the ship with the blue lantern hanging from its prow. But I owe you my story in the right order. Let me have another pull at the wine, and a hunk of this bread too, first. Then all I'll need to be myself again is a sword. The Gords took mine from me."

So saying, Brak tore off nearly half of a butt of dark wheat-loaf lying beside the amphora. He wolfed it with great hungry munching noises. Phonicios and Calix exchanged half-amused, half-wary looks. Saria retreated to the far side of the chamber, safely out of range on a low divan.

Rapidly Brak told them about himself, plus something of his travels as he journeyed southward to seek his fortune in the warmer climes of Khurdisan. He related being caught in the surprise sacking of the Mirkan port, and the events up until he lost consciousness in the water.

"I must have paddled the full distance to shore," he concluded, "though in a mindless state, for I recall nothing."

During the narrative Phonicios had grown more and more agitated. Now he leaped up.

"Barbarian, there's one favor I would ask in return for the charity of this house. Grant it, and I'll even replace your lost broadsword."

Brak's eyes grew somber. "Ask it, I owe you much. My very life, I think."

Phonicios looked concerned. "I want you to accompany me to the palace as soon as you are strong enough. I want you to relate your tale to the vizier. Worthless as Mustaf ben Medi may be, still it's my duty as a citizen of the City of Two Bays to give him any piece of intelligence which may come my way. Our lookouts, as my daughter said, watched the sea battle from afar. Not a vessel survived. Yet individual members of the enemy party may have reached safety, as you did. Your story of the power of the sorceress Ilona is the first concrete word we have had that the Gords possess such magical strengths. Rumors of this we have heard, true. But no one has ever seen the witch work her wonders. If she still lives—"

Brak shook his head. "Not likely, in that storm. But possible. Why your concern?"

"Because," replied Phonicios, "Prince Rodar this very moment is on the nearby frontier of the realm. With the small army we maintain he is preparing for a possible invasion by the Gords via the land route. The ships that sank represented only a fraction of the might of the Gords. If, somehow, the witch Ilona survived and has joined the Gords on land, then I would say that all the Gord fighting men who drowned counted for nothing. We must warn Rodar."

Calix the freedman stepped forward. "The people of this city-state, barbarian, will die for Rodar if need be. But preparing to fight against magical incantations is another matter."

Once more Brak tilted the amphora, warmed by the wine. "Of course I'll go with you, lord Phonicios. Perhaps if the Gords manage to link up with Ilona again, being forewarned would be a wise precaution." Momentarily memories of the scarlet-mist sea demons danced in his brain. "Though knowing what is expected is hardly the same as seeing the witch-woman's tricks for yourself. Still, I suppose every bit of information may be of value to your prince."

Briskly Phonicios nodded, rose. "We shall retire now, lest we tire you. Rest well tonight, barbarian. Perhaps on the morrow you'll be strong enough to accompany me."

Brak gave a nod. "I will, lord." He smiled. "And my thanks to all of you."

Phonicios, his daughter and his steward left the chamber. But not before Brak caught one more bit of by-play:

The steward reached over, pressed the girl's hand behind the father's back. Amused, Brak sank down on the pallet. He yawned, rolled over.

How long he would remain in the city of Rodar, Prince of the Two Bays, he did not know. But it would certainly be long enough to repay the leader of the Merchant Guild for his generosity and kindness.

Toward noon of the next day, Brak rose, feeling fit enough to walk about. Beside his pallet lay a new, well-tempered broadsword half-protruding from a sheath of beaten bronze. Clearly it was a gift from his generous host.

After a huge meal brought in on salvers by Phonicios's servants, Brak set out through the streets of the city with the bearded merchant.

The buildings of Rodar's dominion were stately and tall, washed in mild sunshine. People thronged in the bazaars and public squares. They were seemingly oblivious to the fact that their prince was preparing to defend their lives at the border. Between the buildings down the broad, crowded avenues Brak glimpsed the two large bays on which the mole fronted. Between the bays the craggy island rose up to bisect a vista of the Dark Sea, lead-colored and sun-dappled.

Everywhere people greeted Phonicios with deference, leading Brak to the conclusion that being leader of the Merchant Guild of this prosperous city was a position of considerable importance. A few of the greeters, however, seemed to wear false smiles, and Phonicios was not especially cordial in replying to them. The reason for this Brak did not understand.

For the gigantic barbarian with his yellow braid, lion-tailed cloud and broadsword hanging at his hip the inhabitants had only stares of wonderment.

Presently the two men reached a square larger than any seen before. Directly opposite the entry avenue there was a vast, gracefully-columned temple. On either side of the temple were two towering idols, higher than the highest building. Brak marvelled at the intricacy of the carvings on the bronze statues. Phonicios pointed to the temple.

"Yonder, Brak, is our holy of holies, where the Sacred Lamb Fleece hangs. The Fleece has been the symbol of our freedom since beyond the memory of man. Some say the gods gave it to our first prince. Should the Fleece ever be destroyed or captured, I fear the city would fall."

"No doubt the Gords would like to get their hands on it."

"True, true."

"I'm interested in your gods, lord Phonicios. They're strange to me."

Pausing in the middle of the crowded square, Phonicios made a broad gesture to take in the left-hand idol. Like its opposite, it towered twenty times as tall as Brak himself. The statue was that of a woman, full bodied and without a garment except for a girdle of modesty at her brazen waist.

"We worship two gods here, Brak. She is Ashtir, our lady of goodness and fruitfulness. Notice the great wheels at her base? Her image can be moved by an ingenious arrangement of internal pulleys and weights controlled from a chamber up there inside her head. She is taken to the fields at planting time, you see, to bless the crops. She is a kind goddess. But she is not the deity who receives the most attention." Phonicios swung around. "Jaal does."

Phonicios's voice had dropped low. He made a cabalistic sign, perhaps in reverence to the other gigantic statue. It was manshaped, with great bronze-cast thews and muscles. But its skin was scale-like. In its metal forehead was one great, staring bronze eye that watched the square below.

"Jaal the Leveller," Phonicios repeated. "More demon than man. It is Ashtir the people love. But it is Jaal the Leveller to whom they burn offerings. He is the god of misfortune. He alone can bring us to ruin."

Brak could not suppress a shudder at the sight of the mammoth, evilly-shaped idol leering down from on high. Resuming their walk, he and Phonicios passed near the idol's base. Brak saw that what the merchant had said was true. Lamb and goat carcasses were heaped in profusion on an altar, and ritual fires smoldered between Jaal's feet. Several dozen people were prostrated before the god, praying for his favor. When these moved on, others took their places.

As Brak and Phonicios walked briskly down another wide avenue, Brak understood for the first time the significance of the relatively smaller idols he had seen in niches on countless street corners. The idols were gray stone versions of Jaal the Leveller, about as tall as Brak himself. All had that never-closing cyclopean eye which watched, almost in evil amusement, the activities of the puny humans who passed before it.

Climbing a flight of several hundred marble steps, Brak and his benefactor were soon inside the imposing palace. They got as far as the royal antechamber, a place with a ceiling of gold leaf and a heavy scent of incense. They were stopped by an effeminate seneschal carrying a tall ivory wand.

The seneschal barred their path at the high open doors through which Brak glimpsed a throne. Upon the throne lounged a man of white complexion and huge belly. He was talking in shrill tones with several military men in armor.

"It is of great importance that we speak with vizier ben Medi," said Phonicios. "This man Brak has a tale to tell which may be of value to Prince Rodar on the frontier."

The seneschal glanced suspiciously at Brak. "This lout? He looks incapable of coherent speech. Phonicios, the vizier has many weighty matters upon his mind. He can't trifle with—"

The seneschal stopped, swallowed as Brak stepped forward. The barbarian said low, "I may not wear pretty robes, courtier, but my speech is coherent enough to say that another insult from your painted mouth will get you a broken neck."

Quickly the seneschal raised his hands. "Peace. Peace, stranger! Speak your news."

Rapidly Phonicios told the story. Brak interjected a comment here and there. The seneschal gnawed his lip, shrugged. "Wait here."

He hurried into the throne room. Phonicios rolled his eyes heavenward. The seneschal interrupted Mustaf ben Medi, whispered to him. The vizier, whose cheeks were purple-mottled like those of a confirmed voluptuary, began to shout and gesture violently.

As the soldiers in the hrone room looked on with displeasure the seneschal hurried back out. He drew the great doors shut behind him.

"You heard," he murmured with another shrug. "That the Gords plan a land invasion is hardly news to the vizier. That they may employ a witch to aid them hardly falls into the category of useful military intelligence. Mustaf bids you bring him word in the future of real, not imaginary, dangers which threaten the city. The prince will take care of the frontier. The responsibilities of guarding the people here are what concern the vizier, and he is too busy to deal with anything else."

Phonicios lifted a contemptuous shoulder. "Come, Brak. We'll waste no more time."

Angrily Brak said, "But the skills of that witch could frighten your people into surrender, or worse. If she lives, and if she should strike this city—"

"Have you any proof that she lives?" the seneschal interrupted. "Bring that if you do! Bring specific information about how our citizens may combat these demons you say she can conjure up! Then Mustaf will receive you. Until then, he cannot be troubled."

"Ineffectual oaf," Phonicios muttered, turning away. "Perhaps we'd all better burn another offering to Jaal. It's clear we haven't burned enough thus far—we've been cursed with the protection of a man who is an addlepated winebibber."

With another glare that set the effeminate seneschal trembling, Brak followed Phonicios out.

As the two men neared the hallway that led to the great front portal of the palace, Phonicios paused.

"This way, Brak. I know of a quicker way out of this den of stupidity. Let's take it. The stink of cowardice is gagging in my throat."

Without comment, Brak loped along behind Phonicios. Soon they emerged from a portal which opened onto a long colonnade. Dim sunlight filtered between the pillars. The place was chill.

Phonicios railed against Mustaf under his breath as they rushed along. A figure in a tattered, cowled cloak was approaching along the colonnade. Brak paid no notice until Phonicios pulled up short in the shadow of a pillar. The merchant was pale.

"I chose the wrong way after all. This is turning out to be a black day."

The man approaching had seen the pair, stopped. For a moment sunlight illuminated his face under the shabby cowl. It was a face Brak liked not at all, thin, sallow, with a scraggly wisp of black beard hanging from the point of his chin. The man looked unwashed, down-at-the-heels. He had peculiarly long, narrow gray eyes. Surprisingly, the stranger smiled. But it was a smile of the surface only, insincere and repellant.

The stranger nodded toward Brak. "Has the esteemed leader of the Merchant Guild taken to going about with bodyguards?"

"Stand out of my way, Huz," said Phonicios. "Our business is finished."

"No, not by half," said the other. To Brak: "I gather, stranger, that you must be a bully hired by lord Phonicios because he fears for his life. As well he might. In case you don't recognize me, my name is Huz al Hussayn. I am the man whom the great Phonicios here must have hired you to look out for. Well, I assure you, I won't strike with a sword."

"You'll not strike at all," Phonicios growled. "Your dismissal from the Guild—"

"—was a farce!" Huz al Hussayn said. "A conspiracy directed by you."

"Do you deny that you engaged in sharp practices which disgraced the Guild?" Phonicios roared.

"I deny it completely. I deny it because you cannot prove it. You merely told the fine, fat Guild members of your suspicions. The sanctimonious fools took you at your word."

Huz stepped closer, wagged a long, saffron-colored finger with a long broken nail under Phonicios's chin.

"I may have cheated in my time. But I paid my share of dinshas to the Guild like the rest of you, and you had no right to dismiss me; to send me scurrying along the back stairs of the palace in search of jobs worth a pittance. To be cast out in disgrace is not something which I'll take lightly, Phonicios. This is the first time I've had a chance to say it to your face. You were too cowardly and hypocritical to confront me alone. You needed the Guild at your back. But since we have met, I can promise you'll regret your action."

Phonicios's temple bulged where an angry vein stood out. "Get out of my way, scum."

Huz al Hussayn shook his head. "Not until you hear what I have in store as punishment."

Disgusted, Phonicios seized the cloaked arm of Huz al Hussayn to draw him out of the way. Brak's fingers dropped toward the haft of his broadsword. Clearly there was trouble a-brewing. Hate smoldered in the dismissed Guild member's eyes.

"I warn you to stand out of the way," Phonicios said tightly. "If you don't pay heed—"

"We'll see who pays heed to whom!" Huz ripped free of Phonicios's grip. The cowled man's arm flashed back, then down. His fist caught Phonicios in the side of the head, knocking him back against the carved pillar.

Phonicios groaned, stumbled. Huz darted forward, breathing rapidly. His cowl fell away. In the dim sunlight filtering into the deserted colonnade, his long black hair shone with myrrh-gum. It was tied at the nape with a strip of rag, and gleamed like a condor's wing.

Brak still hesitated as Huz darted forward, brought his leg upward, bent at the knee, for a vicious blow at Phonicios's middle. Huz, it turned out, was a somewhat younger man than he looked at first. Phonicios was no match for him. Brak whipped out the broadsword, a flash of cold metal in the wan light of the long arcade.

"No!" Phonicios was gasping, doubled in pain. "No, barbarian! I am no coward, to have—others fight my— battles with vermin like—"

"I've already fallen far enough as a result of your hypocrisy!" Huz screamed, fastening his hands on Phonicios's throat. He dug his long, cracked fingernails deeply into the older man's flesh. "I won't tolerate more of your filthy abuse, you walking dungheap!"

Clod! Brak shouted to himself. *Don't stand like an ox because Phonicios is too proud to ask for help—*

Phonicios clutched at the hands tormenting his throat. In that moment Brak moved, raising his broadsword.

The head of Huz al Hussayn was half-turned. His eyes caught the flicker of movement. Brak was four or five paces from the scuffling men. Before he could close the distance, Huz had let go.

Phonicios sagged. Huz whirled around, cloak belling like evil wings. As Brak raised the broadsword to smite Huz on the skull with the flat of it, he stopped suddenly.

The dismissed merchant was actually laughing!

Laughing softly, to himself, and mumbling incoherently, mumbling phrases in a strange, guttural tongue—

Perhaps he and Phonicios were dealing with a man who had lost his sanity. Brak charged in with broadsword raised. Huz's laugh rang out, sharp. He clapped his hands.

Where the darkness came from, Brak never knew. Outside the colonnade the sun still shone on crowded streets. Yet between him and the cowled, crack-nailed man, a pearly-black oiliness seemed to coalesce from the very air.

Phonicios held his throat, retching in fear. Between Huz and Brak the darkness deepened, twisting, writhing, filled with weird purple highlights. Brak's jaw dropped. Fear knotted his belly. The blackness boiled and twisted into human shape.

A black, smoky face leered at him. Smoke-hands whipped through the air toward his head. Between those hands hung something thin, something wraithlike, strung with black pearls, ghostly black pearls faintly touched with blood-drops—

A rope! Brak's mind screamed. *A rope of smoke held by a shadow-strangler—*

Brak almost thought he heard the smoke-shape chuckling. Perhaps it was Huz. Suddenly there were points of excruciating pain in his throat.

The phantom rope with its pearls of knots was around his windpipe.

The smoke-shape swirled in front of his face, real and yet not real, bringing a brimstone smell into the dim colonnade.

Tighter the ghostly knots sank into Brak's throat.

Tighter.

The world tilted, swam out of focus.

Desperately Brak drew his broadsword arm back. He wrenched it downward with all his power.

The blade whistled clean through smoky stuff that parted

instantly, whipped away into shreds. Behind the wraith there was nothing, except a thick pillar against which Brak's blade rang loudly, violently, sending off a shower of blue sparks, a hiss.

Silence.

Brak whirled around. The smoke was gone. The foul pit-smell still lingered. Huz al Hussayn was fleeing down the arcade. His voice floated back:

"That is only a taste, my gentle friends. A taste—and more to come!"

He disappeared around the end of the colonnade.

Gaping, Brak rubbed his throat. "I felt—I felt the knots. I saw a face. But there was—*nothing*."

Phonicios staggered forward, ashen. "And I. The face was real, Brak. I recognized it."

Brak felt cold perspiration running on his chest. "Real?" he repeated.

"It was the face of a criminal who was infamous in this city. A man known for strangling with a knotted rope. A man named Yem." Phonicios clutched Brak's arm. "A man caught by the night watch, gutted with a spear and—and buried months ago."

Brak looked down the colonnade. He shuddered again.

"Somehow, Lord Phonicios, the man Huz has brought the strangler back from the dead. Somehow, your enemy is not just an enemy of flesh any longer. He has specters on his side. And—"

Brak's voice became a whisper hardly heard:

"And sorcery."

Chapter III

PRESENTLY A SENSE OF THE normal returned to the long colonnade with its marble floor patterned by pale sun-stripes falling between the pillars. Brak rammed his broadsword back into the sheath of bronze hanging from his waist. Phonicios had recovered somewhat. He even managed a wan smile as he gave a tug to his gray-shot beard.

"Well, my barbarian friend, I suppose we can thank the gods that our carcasses still hinge together properly."

Brak's eyes glinted as he rubbed his throat.

"My neck feels like it's been gouged by human thumbs, not phantom ones. Tell me, Lord Phonicios. Surely there are no marks to be seen."

The quickly-averted eyes of the merchant told otherwise. Barely murmuring, he answered, "The signs are real enough. There are deep red gouges."

Slowly Brak looked first one direction, then another along the colonnade.

"Let us put this place of shadows behind us, Lord Phonicios. I've encountered demons in my travels, and men who were masters of them. But what spirits I've seen summoned were mostly things of the mind, like Ilona's sea-creatures. Never was a mark left on the body by one of them. What sting they possessed they somehow delivered through the mind of the one who saw them.''

Phonicios guided Brak to the colonnade's end. ''True, Brak. Most phantoms do their work in our imagination. Perhaps they even have their being wholly in our minds, who can say? But the ghost of the killer Yem is a different sort. His rope of smoke can slay.''

They emerged from the colonnade and started down broad steps into the comforting clamor of the public thoroughfares. Clouds were moving in from the westward. Behind them the sun was a sharply-defined white disk. The day grew oppressive, the air damp and still. Among the merchants and customers jostling in colorful booths and pavilions, good humor was supplanted by a certain shrillness.

Phonicios paused at a junction of two avenues.

''Perhaps I spoke foolishly when I said we were lucky, Brak. Whole in body we may be. But that keeps us targets for Huz when he chooses to strike again.'' The merchant pulled a face. ''What an ignoramus I am! Speaking as though you were a member of my household. I thank you for assisting me, but this is not your quarrel.''

''I think it is now, Lord. Huz chose to attack me as well.''

Phonicios stared at the barbarian's bleak face. A hostler, coming along with a string of pack mules whose traces jingled with little brass bells, turned to watch a maid in the crowd. He collided with the big barbarian. Brak was standing still as stone, staring over the rooftops at nothing, as though remembering the face of Huz.

''Ill-mannered churl—!'' began the hostler.

Brak merely glanced down, frowned. His eyes were like thunder. The hostler turned white, snatched his cap off his head, opened his mouth to mutter apologies. He thought better of it, jerked his mules to one side and rushed on.

"You gave me back my life, Lord," Brak said to Phonicios, "you and your daughter and your steward Calix. For a month, nearly, the lady Saria watched over me. I have yet to invest even a full day's time in exchange. I will not leave Prince Rodar's city until I have given a month in your service, a month and as much more as it requires to pay for the saving of a life. Now," Brak finished, closing his fingers around his broadsword-haft, "let us find where this Huz hides, and settle with him."

Phonicios shook his head ruefully. "To do so is as easy as finding a single droplet in a typhoon."

"Then at least tell me something more of him, and of this dead man, Yem."

"I will. Come, let's take this avenue. There, beyond that distant gate, is a place which will explain much of Yem, and also some other things which have only just now fallen together in my mind, like the pieces of a broken mosaic."

Brak followed where Phonicios led, straining to see past the gate. "What lies outside?"

"The burial-grounds."

Once more a mantle of gloom wrapped around Brak. But he followed Phonicios with no hesitation in his stride, tall and brawny, standing taller in fact than most men they passed. Brak watched the stalls and booths warily as they moved along the thoroughfare. While his eyes were busy searching for signs of an enemy, his mind was busy absorbing Phonicios's tale:

"Substantially all you heard from the lips of Huz himself is true, Brak. Of course he colored it. There was no hypocrisy in the dismissal vote of the Guild. I sponsored that vote, yes. But we cast our ivory cubes into the teakwood box in open assembly. Assembly at which Huz, I might add, was present. We gave Huz leave to counter specific charges. He denied not one. Only laughed and called us star-crazed old men. Not worthy of arguing with. But I repeat—he did not deny a thing."

"What was his business?" Brak wanted to know. "And his chief offense?"

"To answer the first—seller of the carpets of Jaffnia. To answer the second I would need several turns of the hourglass. His so-called Jaffnia carpets were not imported by caravan at all. They were loomed in the stews of this very city, cheaply. Parchments of authentication were carefully forged. Somehow he came by a seal-ring of the Jaffnian tent-making guild. He used this to concoct his documents. But he also dealt in raw wine laced with water, and solid bronze that was mere trumpery plating. Indeed, he dealt in dozens of dishonestly crafted commodities. True, each offense individually was petty enough. Typical human chicanery. But complaints mounted. Finally, a young bridegroom who had purchased one of Huz's Jaffnia beauties at great price discovered the forgery. The young man's cousin was himself in the Jaffnian tent guild. Huz's victim knew something of the craft. So the young man brought charges before the Guild. He promised to accuse Huz al Hussayn publicly. He was last seen drinking wine at an inn which Huz himself occasionally visited. Then the young man dropped from sight, never to be heard from again. The clamor to remove Huz grew so great that the Guild at last acted on its own authority."

Taking in these details, Brak suddenly noticed that they had passed through the gate at the city wall. They were traveling along a twisted road which suddenly rounded some high boulders and opened on either side onto rolling ground. Brak shivered.

The day had grown even darker. The mist was heavier. There was a peculiar odor in the air. Carved stone monuments in the burial ground towered up into the dim sky.

"This way," Phonicios said, leading Brak off among the cairns and strangely-shaped headstones. "That is, if you can bear to tread among the dead. Many others did, a short while back. See, some of their foot prints are still left."

So Brak noticed. The damp ground bore the faint impressions of sandals and naked feet, great numbers of them, not fresh, but not so old as to have disappeared. Phonicios paused beside a mound of raw rust-colored earth whose upper edge was marked with a small, poor stone. Upon the stone were carved the letters *Yem*.

"The corpse of the strangler vanished from this public burial-plot but three weeks ago. None knew why. But even then, there were tales that there was sorcery involved."

"My wits are too thick," Brak said. "Why should one empty grave attract gaping crowds?"

"Not one empty grave," replied Phonicios. "Two. A second body was stolen within days of the first. Let us walk a little further on."

Soon they reached another, similar heap of recently-turned earth. There was a declivity at its head. It was clear that a stone had been stolen.

"The curio hunters carried the stone off, no doubt," said Phonicios. "The name carved upon it was a name that caused many men to tremble—even though it was no real name at all. Here was buried the man they called The Thief-Taker."

"An informer? I have heard of men who practiced the trade, and were called thus."

"Aye, an informer. A vicious, evil-hearted man. Finally murdered by the very friends among the criminal element from whose betrayal he gained a livelihood. He was worse in many ways than Yem, they say. True, Yem killed. But straightforwardly, if there is such a thing where the taking of human life is concerned. The Thief-Taker, on the other hand, was cruelly devious. And lustful as a he-goat. In fact, those were his two overwhelming passions—a lust to do evil, and a lust for women. Most of the time his craving for women was the stronger passion. It helped make him notorious. When he saw a young maid, he couldn't rest until he'd despoiled her. But his other passion for evil brought him to this grave."

*　　*　　*

A moment passed in stillness. Still Brak puzzled at it: "And grave robbers did this?"

"That is the question I am asking myself. So said everyone. So I too believed, until we saw that—that *thing* which was once Yem in the colonnade. Suddenly I wondered whether Huz has somehow allied himself with the dark powers. If Yem the Strangler was brought out of the earth for a purpose—then might not The Thief-Taker have been raised for the same purpose?"

"To take revenge," Brak nodded, understanding.

A loon went flapping and crying away between the headstones. The strange, nauseating odor in the air had grown thicker. Phonicios suppressed a shudder, saying:

"Perhaps it's merely my old man's mind raising devils where none exist. Yet facts must be faced. Yem and The Thief-Taker did not disappear from their graves until after Huz was dismissed from the Guild, shortly after Calix carried you unconscious to my house. And then there was Onar."

"Who was Onar?"

"A good friend, and a member of the Guild also. He was murdered in his bed. Strangled with a knotted cord a fortnight ago. All—all, I say—assumed thieves did the deed. Knotted rope is a fairly common weapon in this part of the world. But Brak—after what we saw today—I wonder whether it might have been the ghost of Yem."

The big barbarian shook his yellow-braided head again, as if to clear it of troubling thoughts.

"I am no savant, Lord Phonicios. Nor am I skilled in fighting shades. This—" He slapped his broadsword sheath. "—this is what I understand. Yet if your life is threatened, by human enemies or hell-things alike, my sword is yours until the danger passes."

About to say that the responsibility was not Brak's, Phonicios thought better of it. The same skull-gaunt look of anger that had frightened the hostler lay on Brak's features again. With feeling the older man said:

"Thank you, Brak. It is some comfort to know that Huz may not hold all the lucky dice after all. Well, I think we have seen enough here. Follow me. I know a route to the postern which will shorten our return to my house."

They re-crossed the road and walked upward over a rise. There, Phonicios paused. At once the stink in the air grew more powerful. Brak saw its source.

Below, spreading into the mist were scores of funeral-stones taller, more impressive than those they had just quitted. The monuments were shaped into the forms of awful taloned, winged, many-beaked or many-headed creatures, under-world-things who stood guard over the departed. Scattered among the closely packed monuments were round puddles of fiery light, molten liquid that hissed and belched, bubble after sulphurous bubble. The smell arose from these pools, and their yellow radiance flickered in the mist, bathing the sides of the monuments in a ghastly glow.

"The Sulphur Fields," Phonicios explained. "Hold your nose and we'll pass through quickly. Although this ground is not normally open to the public, the priests rarely appear in daylight."

"Priests?" echoed Brak as he followed Phonicios around one of the fire-puddles. Its heat singed the hairs on his great legs. A bubble broke on the surface with a wet, sucking pop. Gaseous fumes whirled around them. "Where do the priests hide, Lord? In the tombs?"

"Underground. The poor of the Two Bays are merely buried. The rich are burnt to holy ash. Under the Sulphur Fields lie the city's official crematoriums. As a matter of fact, my steward Calix was once apprenticed to the priest-hood which maintains the burial fires down below."

Nimbly Brak jumped around another fire-pool. Phonicios stumbled and nearly toppled into the red-shot liquidness. Brak leaped forward, caught him. After Brak had steadied the older man a moment, and Phonicios's gasps subsided, the pair moved on. Brak asked:

"How is it that a man with Calix's quick, lively temper would join a holy order which cares for the dead? Your steward doesn't strike me as the pale priestly type."

"Calix was of a genuinely religious turn of mind for a time. But he soon found himself disgusted by the cult's corruption. The priests have been entrenched for generations. Today, however, to advance in the orders a man must purchase preferment. It's hardly a secret that people often abandon their senile relatives or their unwanted little ones at the entrance to the crematorium, a cave-mouth hereabouts. You see," Phonicios finished, "once the priests fetch a victim underground, living or dead, the victim is never seen again. Once it was part of holy ritual that this be so. Today—well, many say the priests turn a coin from it, and prostitute their honor."

All he had learned on his tramp with Phonicios through the burial ground and the Sulphur Fields served to turn Brak's mood to one of gloom and silence for the rest of the journey. They soon reached the guarded postern gate in the city wall. With some relief Brak heard the heavy oaken gate slam behind them.

Night was falling now. The persistent mist turned lamps and lanterns to yellow blurs. Brak's footfalls rang hollow beside those of Phonicios. He could not get the stench of sulphur from his nostrils, nor the memory of freshly closed graves from his mind.

At an intersection Phonicios halted before one of the stone idols in the image of Jaal the Leveller. The merchant bowed his head briefly, made a cabalistic sign in the air with his right hand, then gazed at Brak rather sheepishly.

Brak said, "Lord, there is no need to be embarrassed about asking your god to spare you further harm. In the light of what's happened—and what may happen still—I would say you were wise."

*   *   *

By agreement, the two men decided to say nothing about the encounter with Huz and the black-smoke strangler at the palace. Still, Saria seemed to sense their mood during the evening meal. She took up a lute for a time, but put it aside soon when her father's stare remained vacant, lost in the shadows at the room's corner.

Brak finished a goblet of wine. He excused himself with a grumbled word, left the chamber. For some reason the hearth-fires failed to warm the house very much. He was anxious to roll up to sleep in the thick lambskin coverlet in his chamber.

Carefully Brak laid the new-shining broadsword beside the pallet. He stretched out. A night watchman cried distantly. Wind sighed around the house walls. Far away, a cedar log dropped and crackled in a hearth.

Brak found that slumber would not come. His mind played with plan after futile plan for relieving his benefactor of the burden of fear which had fallen over him as a result of the meeting with Huz al Hussayn. What to do, how to help—the final answers eluded him.

In their place Brak found himself seeing strange images. He lay in a limbo between wakefulness and sleep. The ebony whirls of the phantom strangler's face danced in his mind. Then he saw the leering one-eyed stone countenance of the Jaal image before which Phonicios had prayed for protection. Somehow, as in a fate-woven tapestry, the two faces belonged together. Somehow, both were part of a dark, incomprehensible fabric a-looming—

A white-blazing spear rowelled down and down to the center of his skull, *hurting*—

Doubling in the middle, Brak sat up. He blinked. Cold night wind touched his naked chest. In the corner, the oil lamp had bubbled out.

The spear was a dream. The pain was his mind's symbol for what had truly roused him. And even as the sound was repeated, Brak closed his hand over the carved broadsword hilt.

The scream of a female slave, mindless, gibbering with terror, rose up again.

Brak leaped to his feet, plunged forward. He was running so fast he struck the wall of the room. Moments later, he reeled down a short flight of steps to hangings which covered the doorway to the high outer porch. He battered at the silks. They swirled near his face, sinister fabric cobwebs. Just as he lunged through into the cooler air of the courtyard, he heard two other sounds—feet behind him, as people were roused in the household, and the scream repeated, knife-sharp.

Jerking his head upward, Brak saw the slave-girl at a window. From there she might have been watching the mist-hung moon. What had she seen that—?

A noise diverted him, down in the darkness of the wide yard below the long stairway up to the porch. Looking, Brak clenched his jaw. His belly grew lead-hard with sudden fear.

The iron-hasped courtyard gate lay like splintered matchwood. Framed against the dim glow of the street was a powerful-looking figure which moved slowly forward, hands doubled to fists, one ponderous foot lifting, then another, head turning, turning—

But it was not a man. Its skin was a cold glare of moonlight on stone.

Brak bit his lip. He saw the man-sized idol of Jaal the Leveller take a step, another.

It walked, with a grinding, a creaking. And it sought something, turning its head.

In the middle of its stone forehead, its great cyclopean eye was no longer gray stone but a bright, white-radiant thing, lidless, fully open.

Open and watching.

Watching and full of hate.

Full of hate and *alive*.

Chapter IV

DISBELIEF SAGGED BRAK'S jawbone in the awful instant when he realized that the idol in the yard below was no specter from stale dreams, but hard stone reality, somehow imbued with the power to move, to lift its ponderous feet as it was doing now, marching on a straight path toward the great house.

In the upper window from which the slave-girl had screamed, other heads appeared. Weird shadows bobbed inside the various wings of the house as lamps were hastily lighted. Male slaves, sleepy-eyed, stumbled onto the high porch behind Brak. One or two were armed with short clubs. Their talk was loud, confused, as they goggled at the stone thing marching across the yard below, its carved head swinging slowly from side to side as the white-fire cyclops eye in its forehead pulsed like some hideous gem.

Other slaves ran to the parapet of the roof. Against the misty moon, one girl was outlined stark and black, tearing at her garments and wailing, "It is Jaal! Jaal moving! Come to bring destruction on this house! Woe to all of us who wear the livery of Phonicios. The god is angered with him, and will surely murder us—''

"Simple woman!" bellowed a voice just behind Brak. He whipped his head around. The freedman Calix thrust through the frightened slaves. The moon shone on Calix's sweating-cold cheeks, glinted on his curly red hair. But Calix had self-possession enough to bring along a short-sword. Now he waved it savagely toward the roof.

"Quiet that mewling female, you oafs up there! The rest of you be quiet as well!"

Immediately, from rooftop to porch, silence fell, except for the last, pitiful moanings of the girl who had been carried away from the parapet like one deranged. Calix crowded up close beside Brak. The two men leaned on the wide balustrade of the stone staircase. This stair led down the outer face of the house to the yard. There, the Jaal statue was advancing in a slow straight course toward the fountain which occupied the courtyard's center.

The fountain's circular wall was high as a man's belly, constructed of granite blocks mortared together. In the fountain's center a carved unicorn on a pedestal spurted a stream from its whorled horn. The water shone like black blood, highlighted by the glare from the statue's eye.

The slave-girl's hysterical cries died away. Only two sounds remained—the ripple of the splashing fountain, and the heavy crunch of the idol's immense feet.

It was six lumbering steps from the fountain.

Now five.

Now four—

"This must be a mummer's trick," Calix whispered. "Often they disguise themselves as the Leveller at the time of the showing of the Sacred Lamb Fleece."

Brak's long braid bobbed as he shook his head. "No. Look how the moon glows on its shoulders. As it shines on marble.

That is not painted cloth. See how the gates lie smashed. Mummers could not do that.''

"Then why should we wait? Let us attack the thing, destroy it.''

The steward started forward to the first step leading down to the yard. Brak caught his forearm, hauled him back. Calix whirled, eyes resentful. Before he could snarl a command to Brak, however, the big barbarian breathed low:

"False courage may only bring us all to grief, Calix. The thing is real enough. But it may have been sent to frighten, not to kill. Hold back until we see what happens.''

The barbarian's grip was so strong on Calix's arm, his face so intense, shadow-stark, that the steward gave a quick, shamed nod of agreement. For it was plain to him, as it was plain to Brak, that if the thing attacked, ordinary weapons would stand little chance against it. Already this knowledge had created a cold tangle of dread in Brak's middle. His words to Calix had carried a confidence he did not feel.

The Jaal-thing had nearly reached the fountain now. It showed no sign of turning aside to go around the obstruction. Breath whispered thinly in dozens of mouths. The crowd of household servants waited, faces round white blurs in the moonglare.

The living fire that shone in the idol's forehead struck the fountain water, causing more weird whitish ripples. From the corner of his eye Brak noticed that Phonicios had appeared on an upper balcony.

All at once, a berserk cry, half of courage, half of madness, split the still air:

"Why do we stand like goats in a pen? Strike the hell-spawn! Smash it before it kills us—''

"No, Amator! Stay clear of it!'' Phonicios shouted from the balcony.

But already the fear-crazed slave, club in hand, was running from the corner of the house where he had been crouched. His tunic flapped as he leaped up to the fountain's rim. He ran around the rim to the other side, raised the club above the head of the stone Jaal. The statue paused, as if surprised.

Down came the slave's club, whipping through the dark air. And Jaal's head lifted, the cyclopean eye suddenly shot with red.

A mighty stone hand reached out, brushed aside the flying club. The idol's touch reduced the club to splinters.

The carved hand closed on the slave's arm.

The other stone hand shot forward to seize the slave's leg.

Brak tensed, bit his lower lip until the blood ran down his chin. Amator was lifted high over the idol's head, kicking, screaming in excruciating agony.

With one seemingly light pull, the stone idol ripped a living human being in half, neck to groin, and cast the shredded, blood-dripping halves into the pool.

And then, as Amator's remains dropped from sight, Jaal moved again. This time, as though some evil essence within the monster had sensed that the battle had been joined.

Two stone fists lifted, dropped down. The solid granite blocks of the fountain rim shattered like sand, crumbling apart. Water flooded out. It mingled with the blood of the torn-apart slave.

Jaal stepped forward, moving faster now. The thing shattered the unicorn fountain with a blow. Next the idol kicked at the rim of the fountain closest to the house. Again the great blocks fell apart.

Up came the idol's head, the eye searching, glaring, hunting its prey. Now it raised its huge stone arms toward the slaves crowded around Brak and Calix on the outer stair. It lumbered for them.

Brak's lips peeled back from his teeth. For an instant his face was inhuman, fanged like that of a wolf from the high steppes where he had been born. Swiftly he lifted his broad-sword.

"No choice now. We must kill it if we can."

"Surround it!" Calix shouted, following Brak down the staircase at the run. "The rest of you men surround it, try to pull it down!"

Over the balustrade Brak saw Jaal's stone head looming. He twisted wildly, raised his broadsword to drive toward that flaming eye. The idol had reached the staircase which was still thronged with men rushing down to the courtyard. Brak's lungs hurt, so loud was his cry of warning. The cry was lost amid the crash and roar of rent stone.

Jaal's great gray fist struck the balustrade blindly, knocking huge holes in the masonry. The idol's feet kicked out. The foundations of the stair collapsed like dust. Brak felt himself falling amid a tangle of bodies.

Men shrieked. Calix cursed. Suddenly Brak struck the courtyard floor. He saw a whole section of the house wall shear away as the entire staircase collapsed. One of its huge blocks dropped toward him, bringing dust and rabble with it.

Frantically Brak gathered his legs beneath him, jumped up just as the block hit with a noise of thunder.

More and more of the staircase sheared away. Three slaves were buried, flailing and shrieking. Brak wiped dust from his eyes.

Calix was vainly trying to pull a fourth pulped, half-dead wretch from under a fallen slab. Strange white light began to ripple and shimmer down the blade of Brak's broadsword. It took him a moment to comprehend the source of that light.

His brain cried a wordless primitive warning. Just as he spun, a weight like the weight of the whole earth struck his shoulder. Stone fingers closed—

There was a cold gray hand gripping his naked flesh. *A man-sized hand of living rock*—

Jaal was behind him, grasping him by the left shoulder. Lightly at first. Then the stone hand began to close.

*   *   *

Brak felt the muscles in his left shoulder begin to soften, fold together under the immense pressure of that awful grip.

Desperately he brought his broadsword from left to right. He slashed at the idol's eye. It seemed to fill the whole universe. It was a white, bottomless inferno, going down and down to a smoldering, smoky nowhere.

There was a blinding glare as Brak's sword-point hit the eye. Brak expected a violent contact, steel striking stone. Instead, it was like plunging the blade into some viscous fluid. A numbing shock shot through his whole body. But the grip of the stone hand seemed to lighten.

Brak pulled backwards, his shoulderblade nearly ripped apart. He was free a moment but the idol reached for him with its big blind hands again.

Two slaves, led by Calix, raced in from the left. The slaves were armed only with staffs. Jaal lashed out with the left fist, almost casually. The immense hand literally passed through the first slave's head, dissolving skull-bone and tissue into nothing. The headless body pitched over.

Calix hacked his short-sword against the out-thrust arm of the idol. The blade shivered, snapped.

Vaguely Brak realized that people were pouring into the courtyard from the streets, roused by the demonic attack. Shrieks, cries, oaths, made the night a pandemonium. Dust from the staircase gritted in his eyes, made it difficult to see—or was that his own weakness?

Brak hauled the broadsword back for one more drive at the whitish eye. The Jaal-idol was ripping the arms and legs off the second howling slave. Brak threw the whole strength of his gigantic body behind that thrust, only to yell aloud when the blade seemed to disappear within the whitish aura of fire surrounding Jaal's eye.

Shock-waves of pain blasted along his forearm, somehow transmitted from the eye through the blade to his body. Moment by moment the unbearable agony mounted while

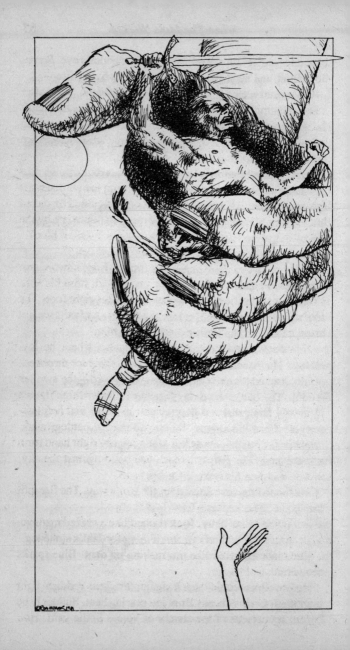

blue and scarlet eruptions flashed from the idol's eye. Somehow Brak had sunk his sword into thick, living fire—

His sensed reeled as the pain burned him again, wave after
wave. His mind no longer functioned. His body, automati-
cally knowing somehow that many more of those jarring
bursts would bring death, gave a spasmodic jerk. The spasm
pulled Brak's sword-arm free.

He saw his steel bright and whole, down to the point. But
violent reddish and cobalt flares burst from the whiteness at
Jaal's forehead. Brak lurched backward a step. His naked
backbone collided with granite. Amid the rubble left by the
ruined staircase, Brak fell backwards over a fallen block.

As he lay sprawled, Jaal began to advance. Brak's sword arm
hung limp at his side. He knew he must stand, raise his arm,
strike at the eye another time. Jaal moved his right foot. The
foot struck the remains of one of the slaves. As Jaal's weight
came down, only pulp remained of the man.

Numbness hammered at Brak's temples where he lay.
Nausea beat upward from his belly. His shoulder throbbed,
his sword-arm tingled. Images were distorted—the swollen
moon; Jaal's white eye looming closer; the writhing figures
of foam-lipped slaves who gibbered in terror and helplessness all around the stone-and-corpse-littered battleground.

Slack-jawed, Brak watched Jaal's mighty right hand form
a fist again. The fist rose black and solid against the sky,
came sweeping downward for his head.

The big barbarian rolled out of the idol's way. The fist split
the block against which Brak had slumped.

Sprawled on his belly, Brak sobbed like a crazed madman
as he lashed out with his sword, aiming for Jaal's stone leg.

The blade clattered like tin, making no dent. Blue sparks
showered.

Before Brak could attack again, brighter reddish light
blazed up. On his cheeks Brak felt searing heat. Suddenly he
became conscious of the clamor of voices in the yard. Hair

hanging in his eyes, he stumbled erect. Crowds thronged the street outside the gate. Men pushed forward in large groups.

One such group wore bronze trappings. And the light came from a lighted cloak which one of the armored watchmen had soaked in lamp-oil, fired and flung at Jaal.

The idol brushed it away. Another cloak, trailing orange tatters of flame, sailed through the air, draped across Jaal's arm. The idol reached over, closed its stone fingers around the burning cloth, held it until it burned out to a black ash.

Jaal's head was moving again, swinging slowly, left to right.

People in the crowd began to shove frantically backward, regretting the curiosity that had brought them from their houses. The idol swung around. It took a step, another. Through the film of sweat and blood streaking his face, Brak's eyes focused. Hazily, he understood. Not why, but what:

Somehow the idol-thing had sensed the great size of the crowd which had gathered. The idol began to walk faster, extending its huge hands before it, reaching, menacing. The crowd parted like a gnarled tree cleft by lightning. Scrabbling, moaning, the people rushed out of the way. And almost as though it were guided by some human sense of danger, the Jaal-thing lumbered across the gore-churned dirt of the yard, out through the open gates and down the street.

A ragged cheer started somewhere. "There are too many of us! The thing is afraid!"

As soon as the idol had passed, the crowd surged together again. The armored watchmen called loudly for order. Frenzied slaves began hunting for others of their number who might have been among the slain. Curious householders from neighboring streets muttered and shouted that an evil curse had fallen upon the city. Brak wiped his eyes, his reason returning.

Yonder he saw Phonicios descend from the staircase ruins,

kneel with Calix beside a slave's corpse. Brak found himself buffeted by people rushing forward to inspect the damage. He tried to fight through to Calix. He wanted to tell the steward that they should pursue the Jaal-thing. The press of people was too thick.

Brak was not content to stand by in this moment of stunned confusion and let the apparition escape. With Calix or without him—Brak felt a primitive churning hatred of the infernal creation—the barbarian meant to destroy the monster if he could. If he could not, he might at least discover where it had come from.

Precious moments had been lost already. Brak scrambled over a block of stair masonry. He thrust at the people pressing forward from the gate. The cast of his features caused some of the curious to hurry to get out of his way.

Outside, in the street, he came upon three armored watchmen. One held a dark-lantern high. They were speculating in low tones about the advisability of pursuing the thing:

"—go yourself, if you've a mind. But swords are obviously useless against it. And I don't plan to risk my life chasing some sorcerer's—"

Brak whirled the man around by the shoulder. "Tell me where the thing has gone."

Another watchman sneered. "Down that crooked lane. But you're chasing ghosts, stranger. Ghosts or worse."

Brak ran, already fastening upon a suspicion that gave renewed swiftness to his stride. A ghost it might be. But a ghost summoned—or sent—by *someone*.

The exertion of the battle against the idol took its toll as Brak rushed on, naked feet slapping slimed cobbles between high, dark houses overlooking the crooked lane. Those who had not thronged out to see the commotion had closed their shutters. As a result, the street into which the lane opened was deserted. Brak's great shadow flitted big and grotesque along tiled walls. He wiped sweat from his face, peered far ahead.

There, where the lonely street intersected another from which a bright glow issued, Brak saw the shadow of something else flicker out of sight. Gray and massive on a wall, the shadow had been unmistakable.

Brak loped ahead, skidding, sliding, fingers hurting from gripping the broadsword so hard. He neared the intersection. At the corner was a house with a dim lantern over the door. Brak slipped into the gloom outside the lantern's glow, peered down the street.

Then he bit his lip again, this time in stunned disbelief. Music reached his ears. The strains of a plucked lute, interspersed with the steady muffled beating of timbrels filled the street. Lanterns hung at each doorway. Brak's eyes flared briefly with understanding. The facades of the houses were gaudily decorated with murals of a crude character. The lanterns shed crimson light.

"Pleasure-houses," Brak breathed with surprise. "Noisy, and open as usual."

He went rigid, back against a wall. Down the street, before one of the unsavory houses whose front was slightly recessed, a patch of blackness stirred beneath a stone balcony supported by two thick wood beams. Whiteness flashed, glimmered.

Heart thudding, Brak ran to the street's opposite side. He began to slip along from doorway to doorway. Coarse male laughter mingled with the music and feminine giggles. Brak paid no attention. A shape took form as his eyes adjusted to watching the dark beneath the balcony.

Outside a partly closed lattice, single eye dimly shining, the Jaal-thing stood rooted in a curiously human posture. Brak stalked closer—three houses away; then two; then one. He skulked unnoticed, directly across the street from the patch of dark where the Jaal-idol hid. Over the stone shoulders Brak had a blurred, fleeting impression of what the thing was watching. For a moment he wanted to laugh. This was worse lunacy than what had happened in the courtyard of Phonicios.

The stone demon, great carved legs and hands still streaked with the blood of its victims, was watching the girls inside the pleasure-house. It peered in upon them like some incredibly shy, witless child. From behind the lattice the timbrels thudded, the lute hummed a compulsive melody, and Brak saw the fleshy blur of a girl's body whirling in a dance while thick male voices shouted praise and vulgar endearments.

Brak's suspicions strengthened in a sudden burst of comprehension. He took a tighter grip on his sword. He swiped at his mouth. Carefully he studied the huge stone balcony beneath which the Jaal-thing stood immobilized, watching the women.

The two support beams which angled from the underside of the balcony to the wall below, just to either side of the lattice, were little higher than a man's head at their lowest point. And if they were as rotten as they looked, Brak's sword might cleave—

The Jaal-thing stirred. It leaned closer to the lattice. How long would its interest hold? Brak swallowed hard. He knew the idol might turn before he reached it. He knew this might be the last act of his life.

Pipes joined the lute and timbrel, skirling as the dance within the pleasure-house grew more frantic. Out of the doorway Brak lunged.

Half way across the street, sacrificing stealth for speed, he saw the stone thing raise its head. But its movements were slow. Brak kept moving.

The idol's head began to turn. Its white eye pulsed brighter as it sensed danger—

Brak jumped, high and to one side. Both hands locked on his broadsword hilt. He hammered the cutting edge into the timber support with a force that made him cry out, so violent was the contact when he struck.

Jaal's cyclops eye seemed to blur, then brighten. Its head dipped as it looked downward at the barbarian who had sprawled on his back after his leap.

Now Brak scrambled up. Jaal took a lurching step. Brak heard a dry, faint cracking. He had no time to glance upward. The music within came to a sudden halt. A girl rushed to the lattice, let out a piercing scream.

Under the outstretched arms of Jaal, Brak scrambled like a four-legged animal. Once he was behind the idol he jumped up. Again he leaped.

Both hands still on the hilt, he struck the other balcony support with all the power of his mighty arms. Though each blow had only hacked but part way into the ancient beams, weakening them that much was enough. As Brak went spilling backward into the street, wood creaked—creaked louder—and one of the support beams tore away from the lower wall.

The Jaal-idol somehow heard the grind of stone above. Its head lifted slightly. Then the wood gave way altogether.

The pleasure-house girls shrieked wildly as the great balcony came thundering down around them.

From where he lay in the middle of the street, Brak watched the statue disappear beneath the crushing weight of the stone blocks. Part of Jaal's shoulder broke away. Then the figure tumbled over on its side, covered with falling granite. White light from its eye flared furnace-bright a moment, just as suddenly dimmed.

Doors of other pleasure-houses crashed open. Scantily-clad girls and men in opulent garb spilled out, shouting alarms. Brak was on his feet now. The mighty sword in his hand discouraged interference. He started to run, back the way he had come. Abruptly, he jerked to a halt.

Broken from the stone body, the head of the Jaal-idol lay

on its side, in clear view. Pearly radiance in the huge eye grew weaker by the moment. But even as Brak watched, something faint, small, whitishly cloud-like seemed to twist free of the stone eye, whirl briefly in the air like some ghostly essence.

Then the pearly patch went twisting and skimming up into the shadows near the rooftops, and vanished.

The eye within the carved head was like the stuff which surrounded it now—cold stone.

Behind him, Brak heard people shuffling forward. He spun, growling. One or two brandishes of his broadsword and the opulent patrons of the pleasure-houses gave up all thought of trying to halt this wild man with the lion-hide at his hips and the long braid hanging down his back. Brak plunged into an alleyway, raced through the dark toward the house of Phonicios.

But his victory was hollow. The knowledge sickened him.

For when Brak had seen the Jaal-thing rooted outside the pleasure-house, a bit of what Phonicios had told him had come to mind. He remembered Phonicios talking about how strong had been the woman-lust of the man known as The Thief-Taker.

Remember, Brak knew somehow that the disembodied spirit of The Thief-Taker had been the guiding force within the idol. Nothing else could explain the otherwise inexplicable behavior of the haunted statue.

Who had summoned back The Thief-Taker's evil spirit to wreak destruction on Phonicios? Running through the dark, panting, aching, Brak knew. The same worker of evil who had called up the phantom-thing that was Yem the Strangler.

In destroying the idol, Brak had hoped to destroy The Thief-Taker's controlling spirit as well; the spirit which, even after death, clung to its old ways, and drove a killer made of stone to watch dancing women.

But the bit of pearliness, the patch that spewed from the

dying stone eye, had escaped from the prison of the statue's crumbling form. Escaped and gone back—*where?*

To its master.

The knowledge made Brak feel defeated. Far ahead down the twisting lane he heard commotion still rising from Phonicios's house. The victory won tonight over the idol was but a temporary one. Somewhere—in his imagination Brak saw it, was frightened—somewhere a pearly-white patch of mist was dancing over the beckoning palm of its keeper.

Now two things were clear.

Huz al Hussayn had command of the magic of the black realms.

And tonight would not end the game. The evil that had walked in a stone idol's body would surely return.

Chapter V

THROUGH THE REMAINDER OF the long night the grim work which was the aftermath of the carnage at Phonicios's house went forward.

The families of the slaves who had perished in the attack of the idol bore their dead to the servant's wing. There, by taper-light, two hastily summoned members of the priestly burial cult prepared the corpses with scented balms and snowy white linen. Wailing and sobbing rose toward the paling stars, together with the creak of cart-wheels as the wrecked masonry and wood was cleared away.

Phonicios, great purple shadows of fatigue showing beneath his eyes, seemed to be everywhere. He supervised the repairs. He spoke with the families of his bondsmen who had died. He haggled with the oily-cheeked priests and made arrangements for the dead. Like the others, Phonicios seemed to want to get the dead buried swiftly and the rubble carted away, as if such rapid action might somehow wipe out the memory of what had happened.

For several hours Brak had no opportunity to tell Phonicios what had taken place in the street of the pleasure-houses. He felt weary, haunted by vague fears as he watched Phonicios's litter being borne out the shattered gates in the false dawn.

Tapers flamed in procession. The families carrying the lights wore cowls of mourning black. The two porcine priests chanted and swung censers. Brak remained at a high window long after the funeral cortege had vanished, lost in gloomy thought.

Toward mid-morning the household returned to some semblance of order. Brak found Phonicios in the dining chamber.

The chief of the Merchant Guild looked more weary than ever. The big barbarian slumped onto a stool. Saria was clearing away an untouched platter of bread, wine and steamed hocks. She touched her father's shoulder.

"My lord, it is not well that you keep from eating. You have been awake all night."

"Has anyone slept or taken time to eat?" Phonicios snapped. "They've buried the dead. And all because of me. Take the food away. Perhaps the widows will want it. I haven't the belly for it."

Sad-eyed, the girl withdrew. Brak poured a goblet of wine from the single amphora remaining. He drained it, wiped his mouth, said: "Lord Phonicios, the blame does not rest on your shoulders. It belongs with that man we encountered at the palace, Huz. When you hear what happened last night as I went in pursuit of the Jaal-thing, you'll understand."

Rapidly Brak told his story. He concluded:

"Knowing only what you have told me yourself, lord, I surmised it was The Thief-Taker's spirit inside the stone, making it move. The spirit was put there, I'll wager, by your enemy."

Angrily Phonicios struck the table. "Then I must take action myself!"

Quickly he rose. He proceeded to the courtyard, Brak at

his heels. They located Calix and Phonicios drew the steward aside.

"Calix, gather as many able-bodied men as you can find left in the household. Send them into the streets. Equip them with fat purses. Have them ask after Huz al Hussayn. But when they have word of him, they are to do nothing except return here. Once we know where he is, we'll rid ourselves of this curse which has fallen on us." Phonicios slapped Calix's shoulder. "You must be swift."

The red-haired steward grinned, a death's-head smile. "Rid ourselves of him, lord? How?"

Said Phonicios softly, "We shall go, the two of us, and kill him."

Brak leaned forward. "There will be three who go, not two."

"So be it," Phonicios replied, gesturing Calix away. The steward raced into the house.

But Phonicios's plan proved fruitless before the moon had risen that same night.

He and Brak were alone in the dining chamber, picking at food, when Calix appeared. The steward tossed back the cowl of his cloak. From the cast of the man's features, Brak knew his news was unfavorable. Phonicios sensed it also. The older man watched impassively while Calix threw several bulging purses onto the ivory table.

"The last man has returned, lord, with most of his dinshas unspent. The story is the same everywhere. There is no word of Huz al Hussayn. Apparently he has gone into hiding. At any rate he has utterly vanished. Perhaps," Calix finished with a scowl, "he's gone down to the pits to commune with the demons who do his bidding."

Phonicios stalked angrily to the window, stared down at the moon-washed courtyard. The earth bore a scar-like pit where the demolished fountain had stood. After a moment, Phonicios turned.

"Then we must follow another course. We must protect not only the people in this household but the other members of the Guild. Bring me a parchment, and the quills. Stand by with a runner for the palace. We'll roust Mustaf ben Medi from his ostrich-feather bed and make him take action."

Moments later Calix returned carrying the materials. Phonicios moved to his writing lectern. With quick strokes he inscribed the parchment, writing an urgent plea to the vizier. The message described the calamity which had occurred the previous night, warned of the danger to the city if Huz al Hussayn should unleash The Thief-Taker's power, or the power of a whole army of spirits. In addition, Phonicios demanded military protection for himself—this to insure, he said in an aside to Brak, that his householders would be safe. He also argued strongly for placement of similar guards around the homes of high-ranking members of the Guild. Finally, he urged Mustaf to press an immediate and vigorous city-wide search for Huz.

The runner went racing out of the courtyard and was soon lost in darkness. Brak gloomed around the chamber, weary in his bones, yet unwilling to sleep and abandon Phonicios to a solitary vigil. Presently Calix rejoined them. He and Brak diced in desultory fashion.

Torch-light and haloos in the courtyard bought the three men to their feet. Within moments, the perspiring runner had ascended to the room, prostrated himself. The man rose, lifted empty hands.

"Where is the vizier's reply?" Phonicios asked.

"Lord," panted the slave, "he had no time to dictate a scroll."

"Bungler! You did not see him!" Phonicios leaped forward, hand lifted to strike.

"Mercy, lord," wailed the slave. "I was in his presence. I gave him the parchment, which he read. But he had no time to dictate a reply, because he spoke it instead. Do not beat me, I beg you."

* * *

Slowly Phonicios brought his hand down, opened his fist. An expression of shame slipped across his face. He touched the slave's arm.

"Forgive me, Dirax. The events of these past hours have left me in an ugly state. What did the vizier say?"

"The palace was in terrible confusion, lord. Chariots thick as flies in the barracks-yards. Men running hither and yon. Mustaf was overwrought and shouting the whole time. He bid me tell you that he can spare not one single man for protection, or to search for Huz. Couriers came from the frontier at sunset. Prince Rodar—" Here the slave licked his lips; fear shone gem-bright in his eyes. "—the army, lord, has been sent into retreat."

"*What?*" Calix shouted.

"Aye, master Calix. There was a great battle. Our Prince was defeated. Invasion by the Gords is only days or hours away."

Calix cursed low. "That's why the lamps shone late. The men we sent out earlier told me that nearly every window was alight. They assumed it was another one of Mustaf's feasts in progress."

"Ashtir preserve us!" Phonicios muttered. "Destruction on destruction."

"Surely there is some way we can find this spellworker," Brak put in. "I'll go myself, to search his haunts, if you can tell me where to begin."

Wearily Phonicios reached over, snuffed the guttering lamp. Weird shadows gathered in the chamber corners. Slump-shouldered, the merchant shuffled toward the door.

"Tomorrow, perhaps. Not tonight. I'm tired of fear, of the darkness. We must all sleep. Perhaps by daylight we can decide what to do next. Today we have done enough. Calix, take the keys to the strongroom. Arm the men. Post them all around the house tonight."

And with that, Phonicios shuffled tiredly into the corridor.

Calix and Brak exchanged despondent looks. Then the former hurried out too, leaving Brak alone and pondering the futility of the situation.

Eventually weariness claimed Brak too. He retired to his pallet. He unbuckled his broadsword and fell into a dream-haunted sleep.

He awoke to a blaze of butter-colored sun spilling through the window. He had slept longer than he had expected. He wrapped the lion-hide tighter around his middle, picked up his broadsword and hurried to the dining chamber.

The room was deserted. With peculiarly anxious glances, a slave told him that Phonicios was to be found in the reception hall. Brak hurried away.

In the corridor outside the hall, Brak discovered Saria. The girl stood near the peacock-silk door hangings, bent forward in an anxious posture, listening. From behind the silks Brak heard loud voices raised in a harangue.

Before he could question the girl, she whispered, "It's a delegation of members of the Merchant Guild. They are not in a friendly mood. I wish I could go in there, but women are not allowed at their deliberations."

"From all the cursing, it sounds as though your father is in need of an ally." Brak clapped his hand on the broadsword-hilt and slipped inside.

Phonicios was facing a contingent of splendidly-dressed gentlemen. He flashed a brief, weary smile of gratitude when Brak appeared. The big barbarian took up a place opposite Phonicios's throne chair. Several of the Guild members, beringed and lavishly dressed, turned to stare at the intruder. At first there were looks of contempt. Brak returned these with an angrily, beetling scowl. The contemptuous looks were soon masked.

"These friends of mine," Phonicios said to Brak, "are Guild members. Their spokesman is Xanril the bangle-maker," He indicated a portly fellow in a persimmon-shaded robe. The color nearly matched the man's unhealthy complexion. A pearl glinted in Xanril's left ear; a pearl almost as tiny as the man's dark, mean eyes. Phonicios continued:

"My friends, Brak, have come in a body to demand that I resign forthwith as chief of the Merchant Guild."

Buoyed up by mutterings from his cohorts, Xanril stepped forward.

"We must act in our own best interests, Phonicios. We have our families—our professions—to think about. We have all heard what happened here last night." Quickly Xanril made the sign against evil-eye. "Clearly, if we continue our association, you will bring more ill luck down on us. You must try to understand our position."

"I understand," Phonicios barked, "that you're a pack of cowards!" His eyes grew shrewd. "Or is it more than that? Huz al Hussayn is a devious man. I could see his hand in this, if I didn't trust you gentlemen so thoroughly." Sarcasm dropped from his words like oil from an olive press. "I could see, for example, Huz wishing to frighten me out of the Guild, so that he might take over by frightening all of you in turn. Simpletons!" Phonicios stalked to where Xanril stood blinking. "Don't you remember the hysterical speech Huz gave when we dismissed him? He promised that one day all of us would serve him. That he would sit in the Guild's head chair! Why should he stop with revenge upon me? Already, like oxen, you're stampeded into such a state of fright that if I were out of the way, Huz could establish himself in my office with very little effort. He could bleed you of all sorts of special tributes! You dunderheads are too shortsighted to see the implications of my resignation—"

Phonicios squared his shoulders. "Consequently," he finished, "it's a resignation which I refuse to tender."

Angry voices broke out in reply. One merchant pushed Xanril aside, saying, "You must step down, Phonicios. We demand it!"

"You *demand* it? You—a pack of cowards—demand it? Hah!"

"The old wheeze about the pot accusing the sooty kettle has never been more appropriate than now, Phonicios!"

"Are you calling me a coward?"

"I am only pointing out," said the man, "that your message to Mustaf—asking for protection—is public knowledge. There were many in the palace last night who overheard your slave."

"Wait, you misinterpret it!" Phonicios began, flushing, stumbling over his words. The scarlet ripened on his cheeks. "My reason for the message was—"

"The reason," Xanril interrupted, "is painfully obvious."

"No!" Phonicios shouted. "I asked for protection for my household—even for all of you—but not for myself."

Hoots of laughter and catcalls greeted this statement. Brak's belly tightened with anger. Men were pushing and shoving to the forefront, eager to insult Phonicios now that he was momentarily rattled. Another man exclaimed:

"Would you put on such a show of fearlessness if you didn't have that wild-haired outlander—" An obese thumb was hooked at Brak. "—standing by to defend you?"

The lines in Brak's cheeks were stark, ugly. He shouldered forward to the man who had spoken. The others shrank back.

Brak's fingers touched the broadsword hilt. "Small men," he said slowly, "sometimes try to hide their own cowardice by attacking men like Lord Phonicios, in whose shadows they're not fit to stand. If you wish to insult me, do it to my face, not via a brave lord who has backbone enough to tell you all to go packing. Though I may be an outlander, without perfume on my hair or delicate soft skin—" Brak's mouth cracked in a teasing, ghoulish smile. "—still I think I understand enough of your ways to answer your insults fittingly."

He let go of the sword-hilt. It clinked ominously back into the scabbard.

"Now," he said. "Who will throw the next taunt?"

"Calm yourself, stranger!" Xanril cried. "Naturally we did not intend to demean your friendship with Phonicios. We understand he befriended you when—"

"To the pit with such talk!" Brak roared. "Tell Lord Phonicios the truth for a change! From the way you all tremble and wring your hands—" Unsure of his ground, Brak was desperately trying to reverse the unfavorable balance of events. "—I wonder whether someone threatened the lot of you, as lord Phonicios suggested. Ordered you to come whining here with your demands."

In the back of the group, a merchant hastily studied the floor mosaics. Brak drew in a quick breath. The hit was scored! He seized Xanril's shoulder.

"Speak straight! Who sent you here to demand Lord Phonicios's resignation? A man named Huz?"

Xanril threw up his hands. "The accusation is disgusting! We have not seen Huz—"

"Naturally we wouldn't listen to scum of that sort," another said.

Quickly all the others began chattering similar assertions of their innocence. But their eyes were deceitful, hastily averted whenever Brak looked at them directly. Soon the protests grew weaker. An uneasy silence fell.

Brak snorted. "Though your words are convincing, gentlemen, your faces fail the game." There was a metallic whisper, a flash, and Brak had the broadsword drawn. "Now take yourselves out of this house! It's all too plain that Huz has spoken to you. Well, you already have your answer from the master of this house. So begone!"

With a deliberately exaggerated flourish, Brak whirled the broadsword in an arc over his head. Xanril leaped out of the way, squealing with alarm. The merchants turned and bolted out.

The peacock-silk hangings settled back into place. Brak lowered his sword. He was almost tempted to laugh at the cattle-like fright of the delegation. But the grave expression on Phonicios's face stayed him.

The merchant asked, "Do you have some knowledge that Huz frightened them into coming?"

The big barbarian shook his head. "No, lord. I merely made a guess, based on what you said earlier. I wanted to unnerve them as they were trying to unnerve you. I only invented the accusation—" He paused. "But now I wonder how wrong we were."

Phonicios slumped in his throne-chair. "Not far wrong," he murmured. "Not far wrong at all. I saw their faces too." He sighed. "Alas, they were once my friends. Some of them are dullards, true. But I know them all. They would not turn on me as they did unless someone outside their group forced them to do it. Someone they feared. Someone such as Huz."

The middle-aged man was clearly disturbed and confused about what course to pursue next. Brak left him alone to meditate, wandering out into the streets for an hour. An atmosphere of uneasiness pervaded the crowds. People talked of nothing except the impending invasion by the Gords. And Offerings were heaped up at the feet of each stone Jaal-idol Brak passed.

Presently the sun vanished behind rain-fattened clouds. A sullen drizzle was falling by the time Brak returned to the house. Though it was only mid-afternoon, lamps and torches already burned bright.

Brak sought out Phonicios again. He hoped to prompt the older man into a discussion of how they might run Huz to earth. Before he had even begun, however, he was interrupted by the arrival of Calix.

The rain-soaked steward had been to the armorer's, pur-

chasing additional spears and swords for use in the event of an attack on the city. Phonicios listened to Calix's report, nodded, lifted a parchment.

"It was a poor day for you to send a love-note to my daughter, steward. I trust your rendezvous in the rain was pleasant."

"What, lord?"

"Really, Calix, things are confused enough as it is. You don't have to choose this time to go sneaking off to meet her, do you? I know there's a romance blossoming, and you know I have no objection. I freed you, did I not? But a more opportune moment might be found for a rendezvous."

"I confess I'm confused about what you mean, lord," said Calix.

Phonicios sat bolt upright. "Where is Saria? Is she not with you?"

"As I reported, I have been to the armorer's the better part of two hour-glasses, lord."

Phonicios thrust the parchment forward. "Then who sent this note arranging a meeting with my daughter at the Spice Arcade? Your sign is affixed to the bottom. There. Plainly, the hieroglyph says Calix the Circassian."

White-faced, Calix studied the parchment.

"Lord, so it does. But I have not laid eyes on Saria since sunup. Nor did I send this message. Have you seen your daughter this past hour?"

Terror came then, spilling into the dim chamber in a sudden materializing ebony cloud.

Phonicios shouted in alarm. Brak whipped out the broadsword again, cheeks cold, his belly too. From nothingness, the thick night-cloud had come spinning, shooting off little scarlet darts of light. While the three men watched, form emerged from the mist of formlessness—

An ugly face. Supple hands.

A dangling thread of smoke studded with ghostly knots—

*   *   *

In the chamber it was suddenly the deep of night, stygian and cold. A nauseous smell of the pit swirled up. From the heart of the darkness through which Brak could barely see the far wall came a whispering croak. The voice seemed to gibber and growl by turns:

"I am Yem, mighty lord Phonicios. I am here and I am not here. I bring you word—"

Almost simultaneously, Brak and Calix lunged.

Phonicios's shout stopped them: *"Hold!* Listen to it!"

"Iron cannot harm the dead," sang the unearthly voice from the smoke-face trembling in the air. "But iron can harm the soft, warm living, lord Phonicios. The soft, warm living ones like your daughter, who is a prisoner, no longer in this house. I am bid to tell you this, lord. Your daughter Saria is alive. She is being held near a certain sarcophagus, the Sarcophagus of the Winged Sword, in the Sulphur Fields. I am bid to say she is well, unharmed. She will be so until the passing of one hour. When the sand runs out, send a single slave to the Sulphur Fields with an answer to a single question. Will you abdicate as ruler of the Guild? If the answer is yes, the girl will be returned from the Sulphur Fields, where you dare not go, or send soldiers, if you prize her life. If your answer is no—I am bid to tell you—*she dies*—"

The last word went sobbing away to a low moan. The shadow-figure began to whirl once more.

Brak leaped forward, his frustration and fury uncontrollable. He hacked at the blackness. The dark form darted away, spiralled around a taboret. The smoke-face was falling apart—

Round and round an hourglass whipped the smoke. Suddenly there was a loud bump. The smoke faded.

A sepulchral laugh went wailing off into the distance. On the chamber floor sat the hour-glass, freshly up-ended. Purple sand spilled down into the empty bottom, running fast—

"We will go to the Sulphur Fields," Brak said. "Calix and I together."

"You will not!" cried Phonicios. "I will not brook your interference when my daughter's life hangs forfeit."

"We can bring her back!" Brak said. "Give us the chance, lord. There is time to—"

"Be silent!" Phonicios shrieked, beside himself with despair. "You are an outlander! This is my house and you will obey me! Now begone and let me think!"

Sullen, Brak spun around and stamped out.

Calix attempted to speak to him in the corridor. Brak shouldered by. He stalked outside.

The big barbarian debated only a moment. He could not let Saria become the victim of her father's hesitation. For Brak was certain that, regardless of Phonicios's decision, Saria would not be returned alive. Unless, that is, she were brought back by force.

Snatching a cloak from the slave quarters, Brak threw it over his shoulders. He hefted his broadsword and set out at a loping run through the rain, heading for the Sulphur Fields.

As he ran he mumbled an incoherent prayer, supplicating the dark, nameless gods from his wild northern homeland.

He begged them to help insure that his decision had not been the wrong one. He felt that he was doing right, that delaying or cowering would only guarantee loss of Saria's life.

And yet—*if he were wrong after all—*

He plunged ahead through the rain, faster.

Chapter VI

WHEN BRAK REACHED THE border of the Sulphur Fields, he discarded the cloak which had been protecting him from the rain. He tried to ignore the gloomy tickling of the mist on his face. The sky was blackening into an early dusk. The stench of the bubbling fire-puddles reeked in his nostrils as he crouched beside a monument on which a stone imp with amethyst eyes genuflected obscenely before invisible gods.

Ahead Brak saw nothing but a pattern of bizarre shapes, tormented black silhouettes against the dusky heavens. Then, looking sharp, he spied a sarcophagus taller than most, half visible a short distance away.

Brak rose, listening. There was no sound save the moan of the wind.

Because of the shifting light cast on the mist-slimed monuments by the fire-pools, vision was tricky. The scene before him seemed constantly shifting in patterns of tigerish blacks and yellow-oranges.

The tall sarcophagus he sought carried the figure of an immense crimp-backed demon with spreading granite wings.

The demon held a stone sword tall as a man in its fist. Beyond, there was a patch of light between tombstones. The light seemed to have a ruddier, deeper cast. Toward this Brak stole.

The sulphurous fumes from the underground crematoriums made his eyes smart and his belly churn. Several times he was choked, threatened with noisy coughing. He held back the spasms by biting his lip until it bled. Everywhere, the light shifted, mist blew, stone faces leered down.

With a trained stealth carried over from his days on the high steppes, he stalked closer to the sarcophagus atop which the half-human shape with wings held its awful stone sword extended. Now he was near the huge block which formed the base for the statue. He flattened his naked spine against the marble. Its touch was death-cold.

Carefully he inched his way to a corner. He risked peering out around it, down the plane of the base. Where the side ended, people waited beside a fire of smoking green wood.

The first person Brak saw was Saria. Her gentle face was pale, terror-washed beneath a shabby peasant woman's cowl. She was forced to stand, her silver sandals mud-scummed. From her posture Brak assumed that her wrists were lashed behind her back.

The person with her was Huz al Hussayn.

Brak's gaze grew savage as he watched the changing light from a nearby fire-pit streak the man's cheeks with a sickly orange glow. Huz's scraggly wisp of beard and the rag binding his hair at the nape were sodden with rain. His long, narrow gray eyes surveyed Saria unpleasantly.

"There, my pretty girl," Huz was saying. "There you see what will bring me success."

Numbly, near to fainting, Saria shook her head. "Madman," he whispered. "It's only a jar. A cheap wine jar."

Sucking in his breath, Brak edged around the corner of the sarcophagus. Shadow thickened around the base for half the

distance to the far corner. Through this blackness Brak went creeping, until he was just outside the shifting rim of light. He went rigid as one of the grotesque figures on the tombs all around him. He was barely conscious of something massive overhead—the statue's ponderous sword, thrust far out into space.

"Cheap, eh?" Huz chortled. Brak could now see the wine vessel. It reached nearly to Huz's shoulder. Its round basswood lid was tightly fastened in place by half a dozen blue wax seals. The bony man sidled over, stroked the jar's curved side.

"The value of such a jar depends upon its contents, my girl. And this one has valuable contents indeed. Would you believe there's a soul prisoned in it?"

When Saria gaped, disbelieving, Huz lifted one shoulder in a shrug.

"That is, if you can call the evil *something* within a man— the something which lives after he dies—a soul. Within this jar, my girl, floats a little cloud no bigger than my fist. Ah, but the power it has! It belonged to a man known as The Thief-Taker. From the way your eyes grow large, I see you recognize the name. Yes, it's the same man. The rascal who, half the time, could not divert his attention from corrupting anything female. The other half? Well, if any creature was evil, wholly evil—and I flatter myself that I'm a good judge—certainly The Thief-Taker was the one."

With this little lecture Huz seemed to be amusing himself, presumably until the arrival of the slave who would carry Phonicios's answer. A fat bubble on the fire-pool surface erupted with a shower of sizzling sparks. The burst of radiance gave Brak a momentary glimpse of another, fully cowled figure hovering further back in the shadows. Brak blinked. Once more he saw only foggy darkness.

Had there been someone there? Or were imagination, fear, the atmosphere of this damnable graveyard playing tricks?

"—when I choose to release that whitish knot of ghost-stuff in the jar, my girl," Huz was saying, "I shall rise to great eminence in the city-state which Prince Rodar is now in the process of losing to the Gords. I'll act before that happens, to be sure."

Huz paused, savoring Saria's fear-crazed expression.

"Shall I tell you how? Quite simple, my girl. I have learned how to direct that little cloud, that knot of hell-stuff, into any solid object of my choosing. When I do, the cloud brings the object to life. I can send such an object on any mission I choose."

Subtly, suddenly, the moment froze.

At first there was no sound. Only a strange illusion, for Brak, of time stopping while a tiny spiderweb crack appeared in the clay surface of the jar.

The crack divided.

Divided again.

Only a heartbeat's time actually passed. But Brak seemed to watch the whole faintly obscene multiplying of the cracks as if it took an eternity. Abruptly, there was a loud report. The great jar literally blew to pieces.

Shards flew. One sizeable one whizzed toward Brak. Without thinking, he ducked.

The shard struck the sarcophagus base. Huz spotted Brak's movement in the dark. He whipped an enamelled dagger from his girdle. Cursing his clumsy, automatic reaction, half-bent and having stumbled forward into the light, Brak was conscious of a streak of white spitting from the jar into the darkness above his head—

"Three heads of hell!" cried Huz. "A watcher—"

Above Brak the barbarian, blackness *moved*.

Some forgotten instinct made him jerk his head back. He opened his mouth for a shout that never came.

Over him, the head of the winged creature on the sarcophagus was turning, creaking, bending down.

With sudden speed, the living statue moved its now-living

fist. The ton weight of the stone sword came arching down
for Brak's skull.

Only the posture into which Brak was doubled saved him.
The stone sword descended faster, racing in toward him.
Brak let his legs go limp. He struck the soggy mud, felt an
immense rush of air near his shoulder. With a crash and
crumbling, the stone sword hit the sarcophagus, shattered
into fragments.

Two of these struck Brak as he struggled to rise. Dimly he
glimpsed Saria's terrified face. Huz seemed equally astound-
ed. Brak had no time to wonder at the strangeness of the
man's reaction. Even as he wrenched himself up from the
earth, struggling to free his broadsword where it was impaled
in the slime, ebony mist whirled close.

There was high, echoing laughter. Hands of night-stuff
coalesced. Brak stumbled back. Between the hands hung
smoke-rope, knot-studded.

Brak's shin struck a low headstone. He pitched over into
the light, a sword's length from the edge of the bubbling fire-
pit.

The smoky head and torso of Yem the Strangler, eyes
bright as the torture-fires of another world, dipped and flew
close.

The smoke-rope closed around Brak's neck.

The phantom knots dug in.

Brak writhed, strangling.

Wildly he hacked the air with his broadsword. Bending his
legs beneath him until he thought his spine would crack, he
managed to hurl himself erect. The smoke-face hovered
near. The knots tightened. Vermilion stars danced within
Brak's skull.

Through mounting pain Brak glimpsed the face of Huz, slack
as melted wax. Huz unable to control his own demons?
Madness!

But worse madness was the sudden clouding of Brak's

vision, the certainty that death was near. The rope his broadsword could not cut took its toll in his throat.

The big barbarian seemed to lurch like a drunken man,
fighting off a cloud. Through his wild contortions, wrench-
ings, divings, he grew dimly conscious that the more he
pulled in one direction, the harder became the tugging on his
windpipe.

The face of Yem the Strangler was incredibly close
now. When Brak pulled one certain way, why did it con-
tort?

As he saw a halation of light beyond the smoke, he understood. The thing was afraid of the fire-pit—

Brak went limp, as if falling. There was a faint, echoing
titter from nowhere. Then Brak tightened his legs, hurled his
whole body forward.

At the last instant he braced his feet in the mud to keep
from pitching into the bubbling hole. The phantom knots
tightened, unbearable, agonizing—

He had gambled, lost—

A trailing wisp of the smoke-stuff ignited with a bluish
burst.

Frantically Brak hurled himself backward. The smoke-
rope whipped away from his neck, lacerating it. Brak collided with the base of the great sarcophagus as another
creeper of fire caught the smoke-stuff that was Yem, burned
upward, igniting in burst after bluish burst.

The tongue of fire seemed to leap and swallow up Yem's
cloud-self, drag it down toward the pool's surface. All at
once, nothing remained but a faint black rind on the surface
of one tiny part of the pool. A putrescent stench hung in the
air. Far away beyond space, beyond time, a tormented soul
was shrieking in utter desolation—

Yem was dead at last.

Brak's chest ached. His mind reeled with horror. Huz was
half-crouched, goggle-eyed. The figure just behind suddenly
emerged from the shadows, cloak swirling back.

"This man I have seen before. We might have expected him. Rather, *you* might have, clod. I did."

"Then it was you—shattered the jar?" Huz mumbled.

"Yes," said Ilona, witch of the Gords.

Her yellow hair blew like the drapes of the dead in the sodden wind. Her luminous eyes burned hate at Brak:

"I sensed him watching. I let out The Thief-Taker, and summoned Yem as well. Now, Huz, you puling idiot, stand away and let me engage him now that he's killed Yem forever. You've neither the skill for it nor the desire I have to finish the barbarian. I have a memory of this big savage, you see. A hateful memory."

Suddenly Ilona's right hand rose. Her fingers were supple, motioning—

"Travel, ghost!"

Behind him, Brak heard a roar, as of stone disturbed. He understood at last the source of Huz's power. He thought he understood even more—an awful secret perhaps even Huz did not comprehend. For Huz was giggling, spit-lipped with delight as Ilona shrieked again:

"Travel ghost!" Right, left, right, left, in the sacred circles—*"travel!"*

Out of the dark behind Brak flew a four-winged gargoyle, stone, alive, sailing at his head—

The barbarian slashed out with his broadsword. The edge clove the stone breastbone of the flying gargoyle. Rocks rained down, drawing blood from Brak's shoulder. Another fragment grazed his head, dizzying him.

His arm still shuddered from the sword-blow. But he felt a sudden, savage confidence rising, a war-lust. He could shatter as many stone things as might fly down from their perches to—

"Travel, ghost!"

A great weight hit Brak in the chest. He lurched aside, twisting to bring up his sword.

The graveyard figure, a carved imp with ten claws on each fist and a horn rising from its snout, spun round and round him in the air. Both hands on the sword hilt, Brak hammered home a blow. The statue split, crumbled. A whitish essence darted up, out of reach.

Ilona cried her incantations. Immediately, from Brak's right, a great carved bullock lumbered at him.

Desperately Brak jumped to the top of a boulder. He aimed a blow at the thundering stone bullock as it passed, clove it. Out of the bullock's skull oozed a writhing whitish cloud. It vanished in the dark.

Brak had only a moment's rest. Panting, he saw another nightmare flying on the foggy wind. A great stone chariot with a many-eyed granite crone for its driver rode the air without support, thundered down the night.

Silhouetted against the sky in a posture of agony, Brak again raised his broadsword, brought it around as he howled like a maddened thing.

The wheel of the flying stone chariot collided with his blade. The contact drove pain into his shoulder-sockets, hurled him out into space. He landed with a jarring thud, struggled to rise.

"Travel, ghost!" Ilona shrieked.

The Thief-Taker's spirit jumped from the stone chariot. It fell to the ground instantly, broke apart. A moment later, a stone crawfish-thing with clicking claws came scooting out from among the headstones.

Blood-streaked, dizzy, Brak lumbered to his feet again. But there was no confidence in him now, only desperation. Ilona could drive The Thief-Taker's essence from statue to graveyard statue, time without end.

Berserk with frustration, Brak screamed curses and smashed his blade against the crawfish-thing's right claw.

The broadsword snapped.

The other stone claw buffeted Brak in the belly. He felt his legs weaken. He dropped to all fours, shaking his head, mumbling, "No, stand up, stand! Do not let her—"

The grave-idol's claw hit sharply against the side of Brak's head. With a moan, he flopped over on his back, gore-streaked fighting arm limp.

Distantly, Ilona called incantations. At once the crawfish-thing turned back to lifeless stone. Its stalked eyes stared frozenly at Brak's body.

Into the periphery of Brak's misted vision swam Ilona's face. Her features contorted with the hate that had dwelled within her since Brak's slaying of the Gord admiral. Her face blurred like a vision in a flawed mirror as she bent down, but Brak knew it was only the effect of his dazed senses.

"I could have sent ten more idols against you, barbarian. And ten times more after that. I wish the battle had lasted longer, so that you might have had your reason, your brains cracked by the futility of trying to fight me."

"Witch-woman," Brak mumbled, making it a filthy name. "Sorceress. Black she-dog. You—"

Daintily Ilona lifted one sandal. She placed it on Brak's face, shoved his head down in the slime.

"Be quiet. Lie there like the beaten cow you are."

Somewhere, Saria was sobbing. Huz scuttled forward, clutched Ilona's arm. The sorceress spun, threw off his touch like something unwholesome. Huz blinked.

"Lady, the hour's nearly expired. I hear a man hallooing in the fog. Sent by Phonicios, I'll wager. If you will stay with this brute, I shall go to meet—what's wrong?"

Ilona shrugged. "The ox won't move, merchant," she said, with obvious cold pride. "I'll come with you to learn the answer. After all, it's this decision by Phonicios that brought us to this wretched place tonight."

"Don't be angry," Huz whined. "You agreed to help with my plan for revenge."

"So I did," Ilona said, nodding briskly. "But the barba-

rian's blood is practically cold already. The sport is losing its savor. Let's get it finished."

So saying, she marched past Huz al Hussayn imperiously, disappeared around a pile of rock broken from the Sarcophagus of the Winged Sword.

Groaning, Brak managed to roll onto his belly, raise himself on all fours again. He heard the hallooing voice once more. Presently Huz spoke, somewhere out in the darkness:

"He's alone, as I bade. I recognize the livery, too. A household slave."

There was more muffled conversation. Brak wanted to stand up. His wounded, stricken body would not obey him. Saria's muffled crying beat in his ears, receded, replaced by the tones of a man's voice:

"—is the message my master Lord Phonicios bade me convey to whoever I might meet here in the Sulphur Fields. Phonicios has already sent parchments to the members of the Merchant Guild, notifying them of his resignation. The parchments should be in their hands this moment. No longer will he serve as their chief. He begs that his daughter Saria be returned, as was promised if he kept his part of the bargain. He wished me to say further—"

"Enough!" Ilona interrupted. "Begone, or you'll see the pit yawn under your feet!"

Brak heard sandals slopping rapidly away in the mud. A fire-bubble popped in the nearby pit. Shadows flickered across his vision as he peered at the ghastly jumble of smashed statuary.

Saria was lying on the ground. Huz al Hussayn and Ilona emerged from the mist. Huz licked his lips, rushing forward.

"I'll chop the girl's bonds. Then we can be away from here." Huz drew his dagger once more. As he leaned over to free Saria, Ilona said:

"No, Huz."

"What's that?"

"Do you want nothing more than the trumpery triumph of Phonicios resigning?" Ilona asked.

"I don't understand."

"Isn't Phonicios your enemy?"

"Of course."

"And has he not already committed himself to abdicate his position?"

"Yes, he has."

A sly little smile stole across Ilona's berry-colored lips. She gestured at Brak. "The yellow-haired outlander has served Phonicios. So why not complete your revenge upon the man who threw you out of your rightful place. Let the girl stay here, and the outlander as well. Let both of them remain among the dead—dead themselves."

On hands and knees, trying to gather strength to fight a last time, Brak marvelled at the change in the behavior of Huz al Hussayn. Upon first encounter he had seemed a strong, commanding figure. But now he acted fearful of the Gord witch. His voice dropped, took on a wheedling note:

"Ilona, when I sent my demands to Phonicios, I made a bargain saying—"

"You also struck a bargain with *me!* Which is more important?"

Huz's eyes narrowed. "You would have me use the knife?"

Ilona laughed again. "No. There's another way. You yourself told me."

She bent, whispered, then drew back. She watched Brak with cold amusement.

Huz's expression wavered, uncertain. Then it grew crafty. Then wavered again: "But—"

"If Phonicios has already handed in his decision, won't the Guild accept it as irrevocable? Won't they refuse to let him reconsider, whatever happens?"

"Probably," Huz agreed, "granted their current temper. Phonicios is in great disfavor."

"Then do what I suggested with the girl. And with the barbarian too."

Huz al Hussayn plucked at his scraggly beard.

And smiled.

And said, *"Yes."*

During that one moment, when Ilona and Huz were grinning at each other in ghoulish congratulations, Brak waited. Then he waited no longer. Like some primeval beast he rose from hands and knees, racing at them, fingers formed into claws.

One claw-hand dipped down, seized a stone. He drew his hand back to hurl the stone at Ilona's head. But her fingers were already white-supple in the firelit mist, weaving a pattern—

Out of the darkness sailed a stone spear. It struck, opened up a bloody trench in Brak's temple. The rock dropped from his hand. He went down, stunned.

The stone spear clattered away. A whitish cloud danced out of it, whirled overhead. Half-conscious, Brak felt himself dragged a long distance. He lay in the dark. The sulphurous smell was particularly strong.

Presently he heard Huz panting. His dazed mind told him that Saria had been brought and dumped like a meal-sack beside him.

Ilona's laughter floated out of the murk. "They will not die easily. Not if what you told me is true, merchant. Come, let's hurry away from here. I want the outlander to have ample time to remember that the witch of the Gords does not suffer her people to be killed."

Footsteps slithered away in the slime. Silence fell.

The hideous sulphur reek swirled up. Brak dozed.

Distantly, gongs rang. He heard muted chanting.

Colors pulsed against his closed eyelids. Mumbling, incoherent, he opened his eyes. Torches shone. The chanting increased.

There was a sickly smell of unguents. Slippery hands gripped his body. A dark arch seemed to float above him.

Then he understood. The arch was the entrance to a cave.

The arch had not come down. He had been raised up, by the priests who tended the underground crematorium.

Twisting his head, he saw Saria, prone and unconscious. She was likewise being carried on two dozen uplifted palms.

The chanting beat high. Brak was too weak to struggle.

The strong male voices of the priests, chanting in unison, thundered against the roof of the sloping corridor hewn from solid rock.

Torchlight flamed and spurted.

A gong rang, a brassy herald of death. Another gong.

Brak's mind slipped into darkness.

The procession of priests wound down and down the tunnel, carrying the gore-streaked figure of Brak the barbarian to the welcome that waited where the inexorable crematory fires burned in the bowels of the world.

Chapter VII

THE MUSIC PENETRATED BRAK'S half-conscious mind first.

Eerie voices in a minor key wailed some ritual-song. Enfolded in a darkness of swimming nausea, the big barbarian listened to the skirling chant as it ascended higher, then burst into a frenzied harmony of many voices, then diminished again, each voice sliding down the scales to a low, moaning note that was like the ululations of a soul in its final agonized paroxysm.

The weird cyclic strain was repeated a second, a third time. Brak grew wider awake. The sulphurous reek and the scalding heat on his right leg, side and shoulder drove the dimness from his mind at last. He stiffened, sucked in breath.

He remembered.

He remembered the incredible duel in which the stone creatures of the grave-ground were animated by The Thief-Taker's essence at the command of the Gord witch Ilona.

He remembered being supported by many hands, and being borne downward to—wherever he was now.

Cautiously Brak worked his numb-tingling fingers. He could tell that he lay prone upon something hard, unyielding. His fingers explored close to his sides.

Stone?

An altar?

Perhaps a bier.

Chill panic swept through the dark of his mind as all details came back. The crematorium underground! That was where he was. It accounted for the strange, ever-continuing chant repeated by a score of male voices. It accounted for the heat on his flank, for the bright flame-patterns that danced against his eyelids.

Brak rolled his head to one side, letting out a false moan. For although the wound in his temple still ached, the pain was nothing compared to the sudden, desperate sense of terror which full memory had brought.

He was conscious of persons passing close by. Head still rolled to the sides, he slitted his eyes open.

Had Brak the barbarian not known otherwise, he might have suspected that his soul had migrated to that Underworld, called by different names in different kingdoms, of which he had heard ever since his youth on the high steppes. Since setting out from those wild lands of the north on his long journey to seek his fortune in the warm climes of Khurdisan far southward, the gigantic warrior had never seen a sight to rival this one for sheer savagery.

He was lying on a raised granite platform. Directly in his line of vision Saria, the auburn-haired daughter of Phonicios, was likewise stretched prone. Beyond her, the floor of a great rock-walled chamber sloped away. The chamber's walls, far distant, were of granite. Underground seepage broke through here and there and trickled down, bluishly phosphorescent.

Between the rock catafalques on which Brak and Saria lay and those distant walls whose bases were pocked with the black maws of the underground, the crematorium blazed like a cruel thread-of-gold tapestry.

A score of bubbling fire-pools similar to the ones above-ground opened in the rock floor. Flames of scarlet and vermilion, orange and yellow blurred and blended upon the ever-changing surfaces of the pools. Most curiously, Brak saw, the pool in the approximate center of the chamber was twice as wide as the others. From its surface, which was brighter than any of the other fire-wells by half again, little licking red-yellow tongues constantly erupted.

Practically surrounding this largest pool were scores of crude wooden sleds. On each lay a stiffened, linen-wrapped shape Brak surmised to be a corpse.

There seemed to be two classes of men busy on the crematorium floor. One was composed of big, generally ugly-faced brutes whose loins were wrapped in linen but who were otherwise naked. They appeared to do the manual labor. Even now, several of them dragged one of the sleds toward the fire-pool. The other group, far outnumbering the first, consisted of relatively more elegant men, all with carefully razored pates whose surfaces gleamed with a coating of oil. These men—priests?—wore gray robes and ornate flashing girdles of beaten gold. Each priest also displayed a blood-red gemstone in his left earlobe.

One priest at the rim of the central fire-pit intoned some words from a parchment. The priest, swag-bellied, exchanged amused, cynical looks of boredom with one of his fellows while he read. The other priest swung a censer that belled out green smoke. Amid the clatter of sleds being dragged every which way and the constant hiss and pop of the fire pools, it was impossible for Brak to hear the words being spoken.

On signal from a third priest, two linen-loined slaves, grunting and straining, upended a sled.

The corpse slid into the fire-pool. There was a leap of flame, a curl of smoke. The priest put down his parchment, shrugged, walked over to a huge pyramid of brass jars, selected one. With a stylus he inscribed something upon a clay seal near the lid. Another slave bore the jar away.

The priest returned to his parchment. His companion with the censer was pulling from a goat-skin of wine. The wine dribbled down his gown. A new sled was dragged forward. The ceremony began again.

As Brak watched this ritual, his uneasiness lessened. True, the underground scene was terrifying enough with its reek of death-balms, its stacked corpses, its destroying fire. Yet Brak had the uncanny feeling that he had been dragged into some busy, efficient mercantile establishment. The more he watched, the more he noticed priests chaffering with one another. The handling of the dead of Rodar's city-state was no esoteric mystery. Contrary to rumor, it was a brisk, if tiresome, trade.

Still, Brak could recall some words spoken by Phonicios. The head of the Merchant Guild had said that those who entered the crematorium, whether alive or dead, never returned.

Brak's broadsword had been shattered in the fighting with the stone imps. He felt naked without it. While he was pondering what to do next, there was a stirring from the bier alongside his. Giving a low moan, Saria moved her head from side to side.

As she turned toward Brak, consciousness lit her eyes. Then memory. Then terror.

At once the young girl sat upright, glancing wildly about. She slid off the bier, hesitated. Then she started to run.

Brak had no choice but to leap after her, catching at her wrist.

"Saria!" He caught her wrist, pulled her back. "You'll only get yourself slain, girl, if you run!"

The girl twisted wildly in his grip. "I know where we are! Let me go! I'd rather kill myself in the fire than wait for them to—"

"Ho!" bawled a voice. Brak got hold of both of Saria's

wrists, struggled wildly to calm her. "The new arrivals are up! You apprentices, bring your staffs, quickly!"

The man who shouted was a priest. He appeared from around a pile of corpse-laden sleds near the spot where Brak was attempting to hold Saria.

More priests converged, together with a group of the apprentices, the unpleasant-looking men in loin cloths. They carried large thornwood clubs.

The priest who had summoned the others was a round-shouldered, sallow old man. He pointed at Brak.

"This is sacred ground, outlander. Harm will come to you if you defile it with struggle."

"Girl, silence!" Brak hissed angrily at Saria, giving her a violent shake that finally calmed her somewhat. She passed quickly beyond fright or hysteria, staring at him limply and horror-eyed, her mouth open slightly.

Brak's belly knotted up as the apprentices shuffled forward, formed a wary ring, clubs ready. Slowly Brak took his hands away from Saria's shoulders. He glowered at the men ringing him.

The old priest started forward. He surveyed Brak's gigantic body wide-shouldered and naked save for a garment of lion-hide about his hips. Brak's single yellow braid was twisted across his left shoulder, hung down his heaving chest.

"We far outnumber you, outlander," said the priest. "It would be wise for you to submit."

The big barbarian spat angrily. "We'll submit to release, nothing else. Stand out of our way."

The priest's mouth dropped open, incredulous. "What kind of simple-witted fool have we here?"

"He is not of Rodar's kingdom," said one of the apprentices. "Nor of any principality hereabouts, that I can tell. Let us quiet him, lord." The man fingered his club.

Instantly Brak dropped into a half-crouch. His fingers

flexed. His mouth was an ugly smile. "Come, bravo!" he growled. "Your club should make you full of courage. If I mean to leave here, it seems I must prove I do. Begin, then!"

The apprentice's eyes, surrounded by thick fatty lids, gleamed in anticipation. The elderly priest, however, raised a warning hand.

"We are under instruction not to provoke him until Lord Nestor has had an opportunity to speak with him. Outlander, calm yourself and—" The old man's eyes flew wide. He scuttled back in alarm. "Name of a name! He's a madman!"

Brak shambled forward. "Stand out of the way."

"I warn you!" piped the priest. "You will only do yourself injury, as well as the maiden if—"

"Stand out of the way!" roared Brak, and lunged.

The apprentice leaped back too, raising his thornwood club. But not in time. Brak's big hands closed around the man's wrist.

The apprentice cursed. Brak wrenched the club loose from the bully's hand, hearing finger-bones pop. The apprentice shrieked, spewed filthy curses. Brak whirled the club around his head, slammed it against the man's skull.

With a cry, the man toppled. All around, Brak heard the rush of feet. Saria was pushed aside. Other apprentices darted in.

Brak met one of their clubs in mid-air. He parried it with his own, hacked it aside. From behind him another club landed a stout blow. Brak felt his knees buckle.

He struggled to stay upright. He whirled the club again, cutting a wide arc that sent the priests dancing backward, crying out in alarm. But the apprentices still pressed in steadily.

Within moments Brak realized his fight was hopeless. Yet he refused to quit. He beat at a naked arm, struck it violently with the club, saw the apprentice drop, slobbering in pain. The bone of the man's upper arm was pulped by Brak's

mighty blow, and the skin of that arm was like a bag containing nothing but jelly.

Another club whizzed against Brak's temple, stunning him. Then another. He cursed.

Two more blows brought shattering pain to his forearms. His own club fell from his limp fingers. Just in front of him, still one more apprentice stepped up, club high above his head, ready to deliver a strike that would knock Brak's brains out.

At that instant, a new voice rose sharply:

"Did I not command you to touch neither of them? Withdraw! And bring them to the blue chamber!"

The new arrival was a plump, cherry-cheeked priest whose ornamented girdle seemed more splendid than those of his companions. The priest wheeled, marched away toward one of the blackish openings in the far wall. Several of the apprentices grumbled among themselves, but obeyed instantly, closing around Brak.

The big barbarian could barely stand, so hard had he been hammered with the clubs. The floor of the chamber tilted one way, then another as he was hustled across it.

Other apprentices rushed Saria along behind. Soon they entered the black maw in the wall, turned once, following the bend of a short tunnel cut from solid rock. They emerged into a small, low-ceilinged cavern where a series of guttering lamps, each with a bluish flame, burned in niches. In other niches Brak noticed several small replicas of the god Jaal the Leveller, and of the fertility goddess Ashtir.

The plump priest awaited them, hands folded over his small belly. Brak's senses were clearing. With a curse he threw off his captor's hands.

As soon as the others withdrew, the plump priest smiled. It was a ghastly thing to see, because it was so unctuous. The blue lamp-flames shone on the priest's cheeks and pate as he made a gesture of apology to Brak and Saria. The girl was leaning against Brak's chest, shadow-eyed with fear.

"Permit me to offer excuses for my underlings," said the priest. "I gave them specific orders that they were not to injure you, so that we might have an opportunity to exchange words." The man spoke with a sweet, silvery richness now. Yet Brak distrusted the fox-glitter of his shrewd little eyes. The man made a slight bow. "I am Nestor, chief priest of the crematorium. When you were brought here—"

"Kidnapped, might be closer to it," Brak growled. "If this be your domain, then order your people to free us. The girl is the daughter of Phonicios, who is head of the—"

"Spare me!" said Nestor with sarcasm. "Of course I realize who she is. Even here, far underground, I have ways of remaining conversant with the persons of prominence in Prince Rodar's city. I have even heard of you, outlander. There has been much talk lately of the barbarian from the north. The man who wears lion-skin. The man who has attached himself to Phonicios's household. Well, please set your fears at rest. It is most regrettable that you find yourselves in our caves of sanctification. Obviously you are not in need of our—ah—rather special services."

"We were left near to unconsciousness at the entrance to this place," Brak explained. "We were attacked by enemies who wanted to dispose of us."

"Of course, of course," said Nestor sympathetically. "It's plain there must be a sensible reason behind this regrettable mistake. We shall remedy the error immediately. That is why I summoned you here, don't you see?"

Against Brak's huge torso, Saria stirred. A trace of hope shone in her frightened eyes all at once.

"Then—" she said softly, "you mean to free us?"

Nestor said simply, "Why, yes." And smiled benignly.

Elation soared through Brak the barbarian. He hugged Saria close, a great breath of relief whistling out between his lips. Only dimly did he hear Nestor continuing to speak. The words sunk in a few at a time, as the chief priest walked briskly about the small chamber, rubbing his hands together:

"—will go free as soon as we conclude certain arrangements. Lord Phonicios is widely known to be a wealthy man." Nestor stopped, looked back at them over his shoulder. Behind his eyes, the greedy fox watched. "Shall we say a payment of fifty thousand dinshas for both of you?"

Outrage replaced Brak's elation of a moment ago. "Is that what you intend? *Ransom?*"

"Since you speak the word in such a blunt, ugly way, yes," Nestor snapped, "ransom. Accompanied, naturally, by other conditions. Once the sums are secured from Phonicios, you will both be escorted to the border. You will not be allowed to return to Prince Rodar's domain during the rest of your lives, on pain of death." Again Nestor turned wheedling: "Understand my position. I am offering you your lives. In return, you must agree to my terms. There is a superstition abroad that those who enter the crematorium never return, whether alive or dead. The continuing prosperity of our cult depends upon maintaining that illusion. But we are speaking frankly here. You will be alive. We ask only that you vanish—as though you had truly been received by our holy fire."

"In other words," Brak said low, "you are telling us that we must pay to go free, in order that we may then hide for the rest of our lives as though we were dead?"

Now the masks were off. Nestor's tone grew curt:

"Precisely."

"Never to see my father again?" Saria said numbly. "Nor my—my dear Calix?"

"Isn't your life better than nothing, you simple child?" Nestor spat.

"This is no holy place," Brak snarled. "This is a nest of thieves."

Nestor's shrug was eloquent. "I won't deny that our cult turns a handsome profit by freeing—ah—mistaken victims in just such a manner as I proposed to you. Nor will I argue the

ethics of the procedure. Thieves we may be. But highly
sophisticated ones, you must admit. For we know the advantage is all ours. Either you agree to help me work out details
of obtaining the fee, perhaps in the guise of the traditional
burial offering, to be paid by Phonicios, or you'll both feed
the flames.''

"No," Brak said. "You'll feed it first, you bloated
leech—"

"Stay back!" Nestor exclaimed, retreating. "Cause trouble and this time I'll deal with you the way you deserve, you
loutish—"

His words became a high-pitched screech of terror as Brak
crossed the blue-lit chamber in two strides, fastened his
angry hands around Nestor's windpipe.

No reason was left in the big barbarian now, only an all-
consuming urge to do murder.

He bent Nestor backward, watching the man's cheeks
purple as he plucked feebly at Brak's hands. Red anger-mist
clouded Brak's mind. He grunted, grunted again, choking.
Somewhere, Saria cried out.

A thunderbolt of pain broke against Brak's skull. His
hands slipped. He went to one knee.

Twisting, he looked to the left. Apprentices were streaming in through the rock tunnel, summoned by Nestor's outcry. Brak let go of the chief priest, came erect, spun and
caught the next down-swing of a club in mid-air.

The blow nearly broke his palms, but he managed to hold
onto the club, wrench it away as more men rushed in, bare
feet thudding.

"Do not spare him this time!" Nestor howled. "He has
lain hands on me—dishonored me—*bludgeon him!*"

Hoping that Saria had taken the opportunity to flee, Brak
swung the club he had wrenched away from his attacker. The
thickest end collided with the cheek of an apprentice, tore it

open. The man shrieked and pitched over with blood cascading down his side.

Brak took blow after blow, matching each with ones of his own. An apprentice's skull cracked. Another bully fell twitching with his backbone broken in half by a terrific thud of the club. But the numbers of them overwhelmed Brak at last.

Fogginess swirled in his mind. Nestor exhorted his men to be merciless. They were.

Bodies pressed close. Clubs rained down. Brak dropped his weapon, shook his head from side to side, muttering:

"I must stand. I must not—"

Like a felled tree, he tumbled.

They carried him from the blue chamber, driving kicks and blows against his body. Suddenly there was a commotion, another outcry.

Saria—screaming.

She had not escaped, then. Despair claimed Brak completely.

He saw the cause of the girl's wailing. A new victim covered with blood—a man either dead or mortally wounded—was being dragged from a tunnel-mouth on one of the crematorium sleds. Even at a great distance, the man's thatch of red hair was clearly recognizable.

The third victim for Nestor's cult was Phonicios's steward, Calix.

The apprentices closed more tightly around the staggering Brak, hustling him along over the floor of the crematorium.

To what, exactly, Brak could not tell. Dazed and defeated, he knew one thing, however—

Whatever happened, at the end, there would be death waiting.

Chapter VIII

FOR A PERIOD OF TIME BRAK'S brain darkened totally.

He did not recall being cast into the unlit chamber in which he awakened. He was slumped in a corner, upon straw that smelled of decayed things. The only light penetrating the chamber came through a square doorway which opened onto the crematorium floor. There, activities were proceeding normally. But three apprentices, arms folded and broad backs facing the chamber, stood guard. They were armed with broadswords now, not clubs.

Hearing a light moan, Brak turned his head.

A ghastly white eyeball glistened moistly in the dark of the room's far side. Brak swallowed to control nausea rising sour in his throat. The eyeball, large as an ivory knob, stared at him in a fixed way.

Brak rose to a standing position, being careful not to make too much noise. He walked a pace, two.

The eyeball was that of a corpse lying on a crematorium sled. The corpse's head was twisted to the side. In this grotesque position, it seemed to watch. Other sleds bearing similar grisly burdens ringed the walls.

The big barbarian's eyes accustomed gradually to the gloom. He located the source of the prolonged moaning. It was Saria, on her knees beside the sprawled, limp body of Calix the steward.

Though no wounds were visible on the Circassian's arms or legs, he lay completely still. With hands pressed to her cheeks, Saria rocked back and forth. Once she reached out to touch the curly red hair of the man she had loved.

Brak was standing above her now. The girl paid no attention. Back and forth she rocked. Brak felt a deep, stabbing pity. That she should lose track of events around her was no wonder, considering the horror into which they had been thrust.

Brak wondered why they had not already been consigned to the flames of the biggest fire-pool. He could only assume the reasons were two: First, the crematorium was busy, to judge from the number of corpse-laden sleds stacked here and outside. Second, no doubt Nestor wished to let the captives gnaw on their own fears awhile, so that their cremation might provide the inmates of the cavern-cult with suitable sport.

Now Brak's mind was fully cleared. Inside this hewn chamber, the air was less stuffy and fume-laden than in the great vault. Here there was only a moldering smell, as of moist earth. Trying to think of appropriate words to jar Saria out of her grief, Brak knelt down. He put his brawny arm around her shoulder. He was not accustomed to refined or soothing speech. He hesitated. Saria did not respond to his touch. It was as though he embraced one of the idols of Jaal.

"Saria? Girl? You must listen. We must try to escape this place."

Saria turned her head. Her gentle eyes were pain haunted. "What is the use? Calix is dead."

"He probably died in an attempt to save us," Brak returned. "We can't let his death amount to nothing. If he was the sort of man I think he was, he would have wished us to—"

Brak stopped. Unless he was mad, he had seen Calix's chest rise.

Carefully he withdrew his arm from around Saria's shoulder. She took it as a sign of Brak's own despair, again covered her eyes. Sucking in breath, Brak bent over. He placed his cheek quite close to Calix's face.

A warm gush of air whispered against his skin. Brak went rigid as a voice breathed:

"Cover Saria's mouth, barbarian. I'm alive, right enough. But I must get up quickly. Don't let her scream."

Squatting on his haunches, Brak lifted both hands. His left hand darted to Saria's lips, his right to the back of her auburn-haired head. He used the double pressure to keep her silent as her eyes flew wide.

Saria twisted, scratched at Brak's wrists in mad terror. Like a corpse imbued with life, Calix sat up in a single motion. His blue eyes burned as he threw a cautioning finger to his lips. The tableau held a moment longer.

Then Saria's terror abated. Understanding flooded her gaze. Brak released her.

Quickly Calix leaned forward, pressed her hand. "I don't know whether we can get out of this place, Saria," he said, his voice barely audible. "If we can—well, that is why I came."

"Speak softly!" Brak urged. Then, to Saria: "My hand is rough. I'm sorry if I hurt you."

"It doesn't matter," said the girl. "So long as Calix is alive." Her joy at seeing him almost overcame her. She pressed his arm. Then her face fell. "Even so, my darling, we're only three. You and Brak are brave men. But against so many, what can be done?"

"Time's in our favor, anyway," said Calix. "We're still

alive; are we not? And you forget my occupation before I entered your father's household. I was one of those very bravos you see standing outside the doorway. An apprentice in the priesthood."

Brak's eyes flared wide. He recalled Phonicios telling him. "Then you know of ways out of here?"

"The road aboveground is futile," Calix said. "Too heavily guarded. But there is another." He threw Saria and the barbarian long, searching looks. "Provided we have the courage to take it. To do so will require strong hearts—and stronger minds. Minds to deal with the unreal."

Brak made a sharp gesture. "We'll do anything, steward. First, though, tell us how you came here."

Calix gave a nervous shrug which belied his uneasiness. "Soon after Lord Phonicios received the ultimatum from Huz, it became apparent—to me, in any case—that you, Brak, had defied his instructions. What would come of your action except possibly death for Saria, I did not know. So I intended to take action myself. I kept your disappearance quiet, and set out for the Sulphur Fields. All I found was incredible wreckage. Monuments overturned, as though demons had been unleashed."

"They were." Rapidly Brak told his story.

Calix listened, nodded, pointed. "That gouge in your forehead—the one clotting over. It must have leaked while Huz carried you to the crematorium cave-mouth. You say he did it with the Gord witch encouraging him? Then that's double reason for gaining our freedom. I expect the merchant Huz had no notion of whom the woman really serves."

"That thought occurred to me," Brak agreed. "He probably thinks Ilona an itinerant sorceress. Certainly it would be to the advantage of the Gords for her to keep her origins secret. But that's getting ahead of things. Finish your story. You followed the bloodtrail to the cave—"

"—and saw it continue underground," Calix went on.

"My intent was to follow you down here. The next round of priests soon came to the surface to look for victims. I hid in a large crevice near the cave-mouth and seized one of the priests from behind. I throttled him until he admitted that indeed there were two new prisoners below—a girl, and an outlander with a long braid and lion-pelt. And both alive. I knocked out the first priest while the others prowled the vicinity, searching for fresh corpses. Then I took my dagger, cut myself lightly and smeared the blood on my clothes. I pretended to stagger to the cave as though in death agonies." Calix's mouth formed a sneer. "The priests are not overly scrupulous, as you have learned. They do not stop to question a potential candidate about his true state. They prefer to accept him at face value—as a source of dishonest revenue. The practice sickened me when I was 'prenticed here. That's why I never took the final orders."

"This escape route you spoke about," Saria said. "Is it a hidden one?"

"Just the opposite," Calix answered. He pointed past the armed apprentices on guard. "It lies yonder. The pools of fire in the crematorium floor are the routes of escape."

The big barbarian's face screwed into a scowl. "Has your adventure unhinged your mind, Circassian?"

The curly-red head bobbed no. "Most of what you see out there—those reddish pools boiling up out of nowhere—are trumpery. Far back in these caverns, a battery of ancient wizards sit conjuring them. The wizards are never seen. But the fire-pools are their illusions, mind-effects designed to heighten the aura of mystery hanging over the cult."

"And the pools on the surface, in the grave-ground?" asked Brak.

"Oh, those are real enough. But not these. New apprentices, you see, are not let in on the secret until just prior to final ordination. By then, their greed so grips them, they no longer care."

Puzzled, Saria asked, "How can this be a crematorium if the fires are false?"

"The fire from those pools neither feels, looks, sounds nor smells false," Brak added.

"All part of the skillful mind-witchery," Calix whispered. "As to the crematorium part—one of the pools is genuine, and only one. The large one, in the center. You can discern, if you look sharp, that it's not only larger, but considerably brighter, and of a distinctly different hue than the others. Ah, Brak. From your expression, I see you noticed it."

"I did. When I first wakened. The great pool is real—?"

"—and the rest are phantasms," Calix said vigorously. "Projected thoughts of those hidden wizards I mentioned. Every pool except the great central one is in reality a hollow pit opening onto a sunken river. The river runs far below these caverns. Where it winds, no one knows. Some say it flows to the outside. None among the priests has travelled it. Still, if we were to push one of the crematorium sleds through the false fire, then leap down into the river, at least we would be no worse off than we are here. A river must run somewhere!"

"True," Brak admitted.

"But," Calix said with upraised finger, "that is why I spoke before about minds strong enough to ward off illusion. Knowing the secret, I am not even sure I can jump through that false fire. As for you and Saria—that is for you to decide."

"Plunge into a lake of flame?" The girl shuddered. "Calix, I do not know whether I can."

"Let the barbarian carry you, then. Brak? Have you the nerve? I think you do."

"I won't pretend the prospect pleases me," Brak growled. "But I think I can manage."

"Believe me—" Calix grew intense. "—there is no other

way. The upper approaches are too heavily guarded. The river may lead nowhere. But what have we to lose for trying?"

"How can we be certain there *is* a river?" Brak asked. "Maybe it's another priestly trick."

"You can hear it," Calix replied. "Stand near a false pool and listen sharp. It roars below."

Peering out of the chamber past the stolidly-planted apprentices whose new broadswords glinted with a deadly luster, Brak surveyed the numerous bubbling, popping fire-pools from which rose tendrils of smoke. The hackles on his neck crawled.

He could not convince himself the fire was false; that it would not scorch and blacken his flesh.

A shuffling of feet, a rasp of voices sounded outside the chamber. Calix wrenched over on his side, white-faced.

"Time's run out! I must play the unconscious man again. Brak—" Calix's hand bit into the barbarian's brawny forearm. "Give the signal. Take Saria and jump through. Remember, it is a mind-trick, nothing more. We have no other chance." Calix's fingers dug deeper. *"No other chance!"*

The shining pates of Nestor and several other priests appeared outside the room. Calix flopped onto his spine, eyes closed. Brak glanced quickly at Saria. Her terror had returned. Her mouth trembled, her eyes darting wildly. A chilly sweat ran on the big barbarian's body as he rose to face the entering men.

He kept glancing beyond the guards, to those smoldering orange pools. They were *real*.

The fire would sear, roast them all to gristle and marrow. Perhaps Calix had been put under a spell by the priests, forced to say what he did—

Terror after terror piled up in Brak's mind. With a mighty effort of will he thrust them all aside. The flames of the central pool would be the trio's destination if they did not choose the other alternative, with all its risks and uncertainties.

Gems glittered on Nestor's hand as the chief priest thrust a torch ahead of him into the room. A sly smile played on his lips. He was careful not to advance too close to Brak as he said:

"We are prepared for you now, my dear guests. I regret that you refuse to be reasonable and submit to my suggestions for ransom."

The torch-fire guttered and streamed as Nestor dipped the pitchy brand at Calix. "Our departed, unlamented brother there—once he was one of ours, you know—may have had some notion of helping to save you. Whatever his plans, they've come to nothing. We'll consign him to the fire-pool also. Apprentices! Fetch them!"

Saria bit down on her lower lip, arms rigid at her sides. Two of the big-thewed men in loincloths marched her forward. Brak went next, head down, glaring but apparently docile. A third pair of apprentices hefted Calix and bore him along.

Several priests up in front began to chant. Down near the lip of the central fire-pool, other members of the order waited with parchments, censers and three empty sleds. Brak peered through half-slitted eyes as the grim group marched down the sloping stone floor on which funeral liquids ran in stinking, snakelike little rivers.

Between stacked piles of dead the prisoners were led. That they were going to the central pool lent some credence to Calix's tale.

Slightly ahead and to the left, one of the supposedly false pools opened in the stone flooring. *That is false fire!* Brak repeated to himself. *That is false fire which does not burn!*

As the procession passed the pool, the chanting rose toward the top of the cavern. Around the cave's rim, dozens of priests and hundreds of apprentices watched impassively from among the racks of the dead. Brak struggled to sort out sounds. Gongs beat, voices sang in the minor-key liturgy.

Brak pretended to stumble.

"Stand up, water-legs!" the apprentice on his right sneered, jerking Brak's arm viciously.

The big barbarian had managed to step a few paces closer to the false pool. *That is not real fire,* he thought. *That fire does not burn!*

Yet on his naked calf he felt heat.

The fire was searing him—

He strained his mind until it ached:

That is false fire!

For one instant he imagined—or did it actually happen?— that there was no heat at all upon his skin. And, somewhere, dark river torrents roared loudly enough for him to hear.

Still, Brak was not convinced.

But he had to act anyway.

Just as the procession rounded the curve of the false pool on the approach to the great central fire-lake, Brak gave a savage backward jerk on both his arms. "I will not die!" he wailed, falling to his knees. "I cannot die! I'm afraid to die!"

He shrieked out the words, striking at the ground with his fists. At the head of the procession, Nestor whirled, stalked back.

"Look at him," the priest cried. "Puling like a child. Terrified of death." Nestor seized Brak's hair. "Well, my outlander friend, you'll have to face up to it like the man you pretended to be when you confronted me alone."

Mewing, foam-lipped, Brak shook his head from side to side. He writhed in Nestor's grip. The priests's cherry-colored cheeks ran with rivulets of perspiration as he peered into Brak's face, his amusement changing to irritation. He gave Brak's hair a yank.

"On your feet, barbarian! Don't show this lovely young lady what a coward you are by—"

Nestor's eyes formed huge circles. He raised his hands. Too late. Brak's madness was gone. His eyes were clear. His right hand held the broadsword he had jerked from the grasp of an astonished apprentice.

Like a white steel flash, the broadsword flickered in the air. Nestor's tongue protruded. His eyes bulged. Total agony burned in his gaze as the broadsword-tip slashed through his throat front to back.

Pandemonium broke loose.

The apprentices charged in, hacking so ferociously that they cut one another in their haste to strike Brak. Through the press, Brak saw Calix tumble out of his captors' grip, snatch a sword and gut one priest, then another.

"The pool!" Calix yelled. "Cut your way to the pool!"

Hell's own work to do that, thought Brak, hewing back and forth, back and forth with the blade. Fighting in such close quarters was difficult. He reached out with his left hand to seize Saria's wrist. He dragged her toward the lip of the false pool while attempting to carve a path with his right arm.

A priest rushed him with dagger drawn. Brak ducked, bowled gainst the priest's belly with his shoulder. The man spilled over. Brak disemboweled him with one quick stroke.

He leaped over the corpse, pulling Saria after. The edge of the pool was near.

On the left, Calix stood straining with one of the heavy crematorium sleds, dragging it forward. Calix gave the sled a kick. It slipped into the fire and vanished.

Brak felt heat on his legs, his naked chest. He thrust Saria behind him, half-spun to parry the charge of two more apprentices. One slipped in the blood of the gored priest. Brak cut his throat open.

Then he hurled his sword up again, locked hafts with the other apprentice. With a thrust that hurt his muscles, Brak flung the man away.

"Leap!" Calix was shouting. "Brak! Leap through the fire! It is not real!"

Ducking again, Brak brought his shoulder up beneath Saria's body so that she was slung over his forearm like a meal-sack. Then he spun again, stepped toward the pool edge—

He stopped.

Time suspended itself.

Brak stood gaping at the fire.

Its heat seared his chest, scorched his naked thighs. Tendrils of flame darted up from the surface, dancing, twisting—

That is not real fire! he thought savagely.

His mind hurt, throbbing.

It will not burn! You must leap into it!

Behind him, he heard voices, footsteps, men charging.

An instant became eternity as he remained frozen, incapable of movement, poised above the fire that burned with a bright hell-glare.

Over his shoulder Brak glimpsed the phalanx of priests with daggers, plus apprentices with swords. They closed in cautiously, shuffling like wolves ringing prey.

Again Brak looked to Calix. His mind was an agony of indecision, terror. Reason could not conquer primitive fear old as time.

Two apprentices had nearly reached Calix now. With a last despairing look the Circassian steward leaped high and went plunging downward into the flame.

Brak saw the curly red head disappear as the fire whorled and shifted. The ring of apprentices and priests was but a pace or two away.

Leap! Brak's mind screamed. *False fire! Somewhere down there Calix is—*

Timeless fear won out, screaming back:

Calix is dead—dead and burning!

From a far, echoing place came a weak but discernible splash.

One of the apprentices hauled his broadsword back to run Brak through the middle. The sword glittered, flashed forward.

Carrying Saria, Brak leaped.

Blinding light beat against his eyes for one infinitesimal particle of time. Then there was nothing except cold, rushing emptiness as he dropped.

There was a roar that grew louder by the moment. With smashing velocity, Brak struck the black river.

Down and down he plummeted, stone-heavy. Saria was torn from his grasp.

The water revived him, chilled him awake. Pawing and paddling, he shot to the surface. The current was swift. It spun him round and round. Nothing could be seen in the total blackness.

"Brak?"

That was Calix, crying somewhere nearby.

"Brak, I have Saria on the sled. Where are you? Call out. If the current carries us past you, we can't catch you again."

"Here!" Brak bawled. The echo sang back, *here-here-here*.

"Your voice is closer!" Calix called out. "Reach out! Hold both arms wide. Try to strike the sled."

Above the churning noise of the river, Calix's shouting grew steadily louder. Suddenly it sounded very close at hand. Something hit the outstretched fingers of Brak's left hand. He closed them, felt them slip off splintery wood, shouted with alarm.

He threw himself bodily through the water. The sled, spinning in the current, whacked against his temple. Brak groaned, but managed to fasten both hands on the edge.

At once Calix caught hold of him. Several moments Brak hung on the speeding sled, dazed, until he had strength enough to pull himself up. He sank down, sodden but alive, on the surface of the wooden craft.

"I—lost my sword—" he panted.

Calix managed a weak laugh. "But I held onto mine. And we're free of them."

"Free in an inky pit," Brak panted. "Where are we heading?"

"I told you, I do not know," Calix said, chafing Saria's wrists. "But already I can see a little. After the bright firelight, it will take a moment."

Presently Brak's eyesight adjusted too. High rocky walls rushed by. Outcrops churned the surface of the underground river to foam. Just as Brak was beginning to think that they might be saved after all, they heard a loud, peculiar flapping in the darkness ahead. This was followed by a wild, loon-like cry.

"Some purblind underground bird that—*gods!*" Calix retched.

On his knees on the careening raft, Brak goggled.

Flapping at them over the water like some apparition from the dawn of time came a gigantic leathery-winged bird-creature. The thing had three beaks, one for each of three heads rising on stalks from a single long, scabrous neck.

The creature's wings beat on the underground air. In its three scaly heads, pairs of scarlet eyes burned bright as it dipped and came sailing over the river's surface to attack the sled carrying the fugitives.

Chapter IX

CLOSER THE GREAT-WINGED creature flapped, closer—

It skated and skimmed the air just above the churning surface of the river. "The sword!" Brak yelled above the river's tumult. "Calix—the sword!"

Spray stung him, beat around his legs as he struggled to stand. He braced his naked feet on the tipping, tilting surface of the crematorium sled. The wings of the hydra headed thing seemed to flap up and down almost lazily, but this was a trick of the eye, for it was flying at tremendous speed.

The main stalk of the bird-creature's neck divided into three smaller stalks. At the ends of each, pod-like heads swayed, containing those immense scarlet eyes. The three heads came closer together, then shot forward as one when the hydra-bird neared the sled.

White-cheeked, Calix clutched Saria against him. Brak balanced precariously on the uneven surface, poised his sword. The huge bird was almost upon them.

All three of its beaks were open revealing a sticky-scarlet

maw in each head. The beaks looked cruelly sharp. They clicked steadily and noisily. The bird swept lower—

Brak lopped at the left head, felt the broadsword sever leathery flesh.

The head dropped into the racing water. Brak's lips peeled back in a humorless wolf-smile while the bird shot on. He screwed his head around, watched the bird wheel. He shouted above the water's noise:

"That stroke may be enough to drive it away—"

Words caught in his throat. The hydra-bird, flapping a trifle erratically a moment ago, had wheeled again, was skimming back along the high-vaulted underground channel. And at the end of the severed, ichor-dripping neck stalk, a sickly pink bud-like thing swelled—swelled—*and budded suddenly into a new, full-grown head with clicking beak*.

A sickened sob shook Brak's chest as he braced himself again. How long could he stand against a creature that could re-create parts of itself from its own gore?

Louder the wings beat, louder than the river's rushing. The air darkened above Brak as the hydra-bird dipped again. Its reddish lantern eyes searched for the puny human thing that had struck it the first time. Maddened, Brak ripped the air with the broadsword.

This time the blade cleft through one of the necks, then another. The third head shot down and as the bird winged by, its beak clicked savagely on Brak's forearm, tearing out a gobbet of flesh.

On the surface of the sled, one of the bird's fallen heads twitched. The beak was still clicking frantically, but the reddish glow was dying out of the now-milky eyes.

Brak's shoulders and torso were sticky with the foul-smelling ichor that had sprayed from the severed necks. Necks which, even as he watched, budded and put forth new beaked heads as the hydra-bird completed its next turn.

"The sled is racing too fast," Brak yelled to Calix. "All this pitching—I can't strike properly."

"What good will it do?" Calix shouted back. "The thing is unkillable!"

"Is the current growing swifter?" Brak bawled. Calix gave a frightened nod.

Brak's thews ached from the strain of standing spraddle-legged on the treacherous sled surface. Once more the hydra-bird was drawing close. Its immense wings spread across the entire width of the broad underground river. They made the air churn with their motion. Brak crouched down as the winged juggernaut sped over him, suddenly going into a sharp turn, its wings flapping more loudly than ever.

One of the beaked heads darted at Brak. He hacked at it. The sled pitched dangerously. The blow missed. The beaked head shot on past Brak, questing for Saria huddled against Calix.

Brak leaped forward, wrapped his elbow around the sinuous neck. Another beak pecked at his spine. Brak concentrated on the thing writhing in his grasp.

The head swung around until Brak's face was no more than a hand's width from the swollen red eyes. Each eye was nearly half as high as Brak himself. A rotting smell spewed out of the thing's maw as it opened its beak to devour Brak's shoulder.

The barbarian wrenched his arm back far as it would go, then rammed it forward. Shining steel slid down the bird's throat. Brak twisted the blade wildly. It emerged from the soft head wall. Brak jerked back. The blade sliced the head open along one side.

Ichor rained on him, mingling with the spume thrown up over the edge of the sled. The cavern walls shot by in a continuous blur. Brak ducked out from under the beak of the second head darting at him from behind. He pinned the first neck to the surface of the sled with his free hand, used his sword to deliver a short, chopping blow that severed the head completely.

With another of its eerie, loon-like wails, the hydra-bird flapped into retreat.

Brak rubbed at his wound. He was a ghastly sight as he tottered on the sled, slimed with a mixture of blood, ichor and spray. The creature's polyp-head was budding again as the bird rose up to the ceiling of the cavern. It hung suspended there a moment, its wings beating, beating steadily.

"Keep the girl's face down," Brak shouted as the sled pitched along, clearly out of control. "The thing means to make another attack—"

Just as he spoke, the bird uncoiled itself from the cavern roof and arrowed down at the fugitives.

All three heads projected far out, and were held close together. Brak would have a difficult time getting around the massed heads to strike at the three necks. He watched the eyes loom larger, larger—

He braced himself for the onslaught by clamping both hands on his sword hilt. Faster the hydra-bird dropped, faster—

It levelled out when it neared the water. All three heads were pressed tightly together now. All three beaks clicked in unison. Brak hauled his broadsword back over his head, started the downswing, and felt the sled pitch violently under him.

His sword sliced empty air. His feet slipped from beneath him. With a cry he landed on his back atop Calix and Saria. He clutched his sword helplessly as the bird-heads drove at them, separating slightly, one darting after Calix, another after the girl, the third after Brak.

The sharp beak closed over Brak's thigh, bit deep. Shrieking a savage cry of agony, Brak rammed his blade up and over, into the creature's left eyesocket. There was a sudden scarlet flare within the eye. But the beak did not release. It bit deeper. Calix cursed and battered at the head attacking him. Saria moaned—

A mighty crash wiped out every other sensation.

Brak was pitched this way, that. The sled threatened to overturn. The loon-like wail rose up to a chilling peak, accompanied by a thrashing of wings. Brak was barely able to grip the sword-hilt hard enough to pull it free of the gutted eye. Water cascaded over him, choking him. Abruptly, there was a peculiar silence.

The tenor of the water's rush dropped, became more even. On his cheeks, which stung from the touch of the droplets of ichor, Brak felt a rush of air that was somehow different. Cooler, and sweeter.

Tiny lights flared high overhead. Brak peered at them as the sled's speed slackened. Calix was on his knees, looking backward the way they had come. What they saw was a sheer rock cliff with a small, dark opening down near the water's surface.

From this opening, the river gushed into the open air.

Lost but a moment ago, Brak found it within himself to laugh weakly. He laid the broadsword down between his knees as the speed of the sled decreased even more.

"That crash we heard," he panted. "The winged monster struck the cavern wall, while we shot on through the small opening. That is all that saved us, Calix."

"But saved we are," the Circassian practically crowed. He was half-crying, half-laughing. "If it hadn't been for you, Brak, holding off the creature so long, we wouldn't be alive at all."

"I couldn't have done it much more," Brak gasped. "But we've finished with it. It can go back to the dark place where it nests. You were right, Calix, about the river emerging aboveground. But where are we?"

Tenderly Calix bent over Saria. He rubbed her hands until she came out of the shocked state into which fright had driven her. Brak slapped a strand of hair back from his forehead. He found it difficult to control his trembling, and he breathed in great sucking gulps.

The sled slowed still further.

Up ahead, the river turned. But it was impossible to discover their whereabouts, for the stream was flanked on both sides by banks twice as tall as Brak. A few diamond-white stars had emerged. There was a ruddy glow just above the lip of the left-hand bank, indicating twilight.

Soon the current twisted the sled in toward shore. Brak grasped an immense half-shrunken root. Presently the sled nudged against the steep bank, no longer troubled by the current. Climbing up, Brak took Saria by the hand.

"Are you all right, girl? Have you strength to walk?"

"Yes. Yes, I think so. With clean air to breathe, things are better," she murmured dully.

Brak nodded. He went clammering ahead up the slope, eager to reach the top. The glare of the red-colored sundown light increased. Cautiously he pulled himself over the rim, parted some faintly clammy reeds, caught his breath.

"Hurry, Calix," he shouted down. "I think we must be outside the city. But for the rest—"

His eyes swept the horizon, trying to pull meaning from the jumble of shapes in movement all across the broad plain. In a moment, Saria and the steward were beside him.

To their left, great rock ramparts rose up. Behind them rear tall buildings reminiscent of the architecture of Prince Rodar's city. Long lines of men in armor were streaming in from the plain, rushing toward a tall gate in the wall.

Toward the plain's center, fires smoldered. Brak thought he saw a broken chariot wheel revolving. A battle-pennon on a staff fluttered in the smoke. The air was filled with faint cries of pain. Armored corpses lay everywhere.

In a hushed voice Calix said, "Look yonder, Brak. On the ridge. What are those machines?"

Brak swung his head to the right. Again he gasped.

Silhouetted on the rise against the ruddy glare of sunset were the black outlines of horse-drawn war chariots, a hundred of them at minimum. From each side of the slow-moving vehicles projected long devices like swords, three of them per side. They revolved, as if attached to the chariot-wheels.

"No machines like that have ever been seen in Rodar's armory," Calix said, standing up. "Everything I see tells me we've come upon a battlefield. A battlefield on which things have gone badly for the Prince's people. Look at the way the lines of men run toward the gates. That spells a retreat. We'd best get ourselves inside the walls too."

So saying, he leaped to his feet. Holding Saria's hand, he began to run across the plain. The prospect of gaining sanctuary lent the girl strength. Brak loped along behind them.

Soon they reached the first of the corpses. Hastily Calix pulled Saria's head down against his shoulder. The warm, rich smell of blood blew on the night wind, mingling with the shouts and the blast of trumpets.

Calix swallowed violently. "Brak, these men were not speared. Neither were they arrowed down."

"They were hacked into pieces of meat." Brak kicked a gory leg aside. His stomach wrenched. "Now I know of what those chariots remind me. More particularly, the strange revolving objects projecting from their wheels."

He swung, staring at the slow black-etched cavalcade which was crawling slowly along the sunset-hued rise.

"Those chariots carry scythes on their wheels."

Calix urged Saria forward again, letting her walk as best she could. To hide from the sight of mutilated corpses and dismembered limbs was practically impossible, so numerous were they. Brak had dwelled long enough with Phonicios to recognize the trappings strewn with the dead. Here and there, a shield bearing an image of the goat-god of the Gords glittered in the wan sunset. But for every Gord warrior slain, dozens of Rodar's troops lay butchered.

Within a short time, Brak and his companions reached the main road. The last straggling soldiers were hurrying toward the lamp-lit gates. No one paid the three fugitives the slightest bit of attention. Brak ran ahead until he caught up with a young soldier, fell into step beside him.

"The Gords had the best of this one, eh?" he rumbled.

The soldier turned. He gawked at Brak's towering stature, bloody appearance, shrugged weakly.

"What are men with conventional armor against those scythe-chariots? The men in the way of the revolving blades never had a chance. We lost fifty to every one of the Gords who fell."

"But surely Prince Rodar will be able to hold the army together."

"Then you didn't hear the news?"

"It seems I didn't. Tell me."

"The couriers say Prince Rodar was killed at the frontier. His army was totally routed late last night by the same scythe-chariots which swept down here at high noon. No one saw Rodar fall, but his standard was found broken and trampled. That spells the end. Besides, now the buffoon Mustaf ben Medi is in command. I fancy you never saw *him* today."

Brak shook his head. The soldier spat.

"Nor did I, or anyone else. He stayed within the walls."

The soldier glanced over his shoulder at the line of scythe-chariots which had come to a standstill on the horizon.

"Well, they've decided to let us alone tonight. No doubt they want us properly fatted when they attack the city tomorrow and kill us all." So saying, he made the sign against evil eye and hurried ahead.

Brak dropped back to his companions. Rapidly he reported all he had learned, finishing:

As soon as we are within the gates, Calix, we should take the girl to her father's house. Then, I suppose, they will want every able-bodied man to defend the walls. Clearly there'll be a siege."

Limping along and panting with exhaustion, Calix said,

"Brak, you could ride out if you wanted. This is not your war."

Thinking of the connection between the fierce Gords and their witch Ilona and Huz al Hussayn, Brak glowered. "It has become my war, Circassian."

Soon they passed beneath the arch of the great gate. An immense crowd of soldiers and citizenry milled just within, filling a public square from side to side. Tall buildings surrounded the square. Brak and Calix had difficulty pushing through toward a street which would take them to the house of Phonicios.

Final stragglers from the beaten army, most with severe wounds, staggered through the gates, adding to the crowd. Torches blazed and streamed as the last sundown light leaked from the sky. Great winches creaked. The mighty gates groaned shut.

On pulleys a huge timber as thick as Brak's chest was lowered from high overhead. It settled into upright iron prongs with a tremendous chunking sound. At once, an audible sigh of relief could be heard from the crowd.

Shoving along, Brak said over his shoulder, "The crowd seems ill-disposed to move. What can they be waiting for?"

Saria's pointing hand provided the answer. "Look, both of you. Heralds, on that balcony."

On the far side of the square, six liveried men carrying slender horns of brass had appeared. They raised the horns and blew a long, sustained note.

Immediately, like a ghostly echo from the hills outside the city, came the sound of notes blown on warhorns, in defiant response.

A figure emerged on the balcony. He gestured to the crowd for quiet. There was some cheering and applause, but not much.

"I recognize that pot shape," Calix said between his teeth. "Gods of the blackness! He's put on the crested helmet. That means Prince Rodar is dead."

"Citizens! Citizens, your attention!" cried the man on the balcony, gesturing more violently. Brak folded his brawny arms across his chest. He was pressed on all sides by soldiers and commoners. He felt uneasy. So did the crowd. The soldiers whispered to one another. Fear seemed to gather like a cloud over the square.

"Citizens!" Mustaf brayed from the balcony over the heads of the multitude. "There is no reason to fear the Gords. We suffered loss and desolation on the field today, true—"

"Where were you, pudding-belly?" a voice cried. No one laughed.

Mustaf hitched up his baldric which was weighted with a ceremonial sword whose gem studding even at long distance dazzled the eye. "Let the Gords with their scythe-machines gather on the hills tonight!" he shouted. "Let them blow their war trumpets in derision! They will be defeated when they try to storm us behind these walls. I promise you that much, my people. Now that news has reached us of the death of our illustrious Prince, I will take command. I swear before Ashtir and Jaal the Leveller that we shall win."

Another voice cried out, "How? Tell us how! Will we attack the Gords with lofty pronouncements?"

"Stop your yapping tongues and I will tell you how!"

There was an hysterical edge in the vizier's voice, Brak thought. Yet perhaps it was only a trick of wind, or the result of voices rebounding between the great buildings fronting the square. Gradually the mutterings died away. A last few whispers were stilled by angry shushes from neighbors. Mustaf ben Medi gripped the balcony rail. Several other splendidly-armored officials had emerged behind him to listen attentively. Mustaf's voice carried all the way to the outer walls:

"The Gords have their scythe-chariots, which are new and frightening machines. But they are not half so frightening as the weapon which I have uncovered within this very city. The weapon which brings the might of the gods themselves to our defense.''

The words were enough to start people whispering again. A horsejawed foot soldier nearby grumbled, ''Mustaf signing a pact with the masters of the pit, is he? Give me troops, not magic!''

But others were less cynical. On every hand, Brak heard hushed assurances that Mustaf had somehow supplicated Ashtir or, more probably, Jaal the Leveller, and received omens of a victory.

''What's this weapon of yours vizier?'' the cry went up.

''Yes! Tell us!''

''What is the weapon?''

''When will we see it?''

''You will see it when the Gords lay siege to our walls!'' Mustaf cried back. ''They will flee with their eyes unbelieving and their bowels knotted in terror.'' Mustaf threw his arms wide. His voice was a scream of supplication: ''Believe me! You have nothing to fear! The gods are on our side. The gods will *prove* it so!''

''Prove it so?'' the whisper ran. ''The gods will prove it so? How? *How?*''

All at once, the crowd's mood changed. Like talismans, words passed from mouth to mouth:

''Have no fear. The gods will prove it so.''

Puzzled, the big barbarian suddenly glanced to the balcony again. An officer in royal trappings was leaning forward to speak to Mustaf. Brak stiffened. Even at a great distance, the narrow face with its tied hair and scraggly beard was recognizable.

The man, wearing ceremonial armor and present in the vizier's own party, was Huz al Hussayn.

Now Brak's suspicion became certainty. If Huz had offered the services of his demon-forces to Mustaf—for what else could account for the vizier's claim of a quasimagical weapon?—then Brak felt positive that neither Huz nor Mustaf knew that the witch who made the spirits obey her was a servant of the Gods. Huz had advanced himself, right enough. But at a price he could not guess—the betrayal of an entire city into the hands of a woman who was the enemy.

No other explanation could account for Huz's presence in the royal party, for Mustaf's confidence, Brak believed. Unknowing, Huz would lead Prince Rodar's people to destruction.

"Calix?" Brak called. "Take the girl to her father! I must speak to the vizier at once.".

Before Calix could reply, Brak went shouldering through the crowd, angry-eyed.

Before he had half crossed the public square, he looked up. So did a thousand others, gaping.

A great ball of fire whizzed over the wall. It struck the face of one of the buildings, raining down tendrils of flame. Shrieking people fled in panic.

At once, Mustaf, Huz and the other nobles vanished from the balcony. Suddenly a whip cracked, twining itself around the barbarian's middle,

An officer mounted on horseback snaked the whip loose, shouted at Brak:

"You—and all the rest of you able-bodied men gawking there! To the walls! The Gords have not chosen to wait till dawn. We are being attacked!"

Chapter X

THE SHOD HOOFS OF THE OFFICER'S mount struck fire from the cobbles of the square as he attempted to ride on. He cracked his lash over the backs of the citizens.

"Women and children to the houses! Men to the walls! The Gords are attacking!"

All around the big barbarian, people began to thrust and shove. Wails of terrified children blended with the sharp poppings of the whips Mustaf's officers were using to drive the reluctant males toward ladders which led up to the battle ramparts at the top of the mighty walls. Another firepot came arching through the black heavens.

A hundred men and women fled from beneath it. Many of them ran too slowly. The fireball struck. Brak choked in horror at the sight of dozens of human beings engulfed in a bath of hell-bright flame. Like condemned souls writhing in torment, the people disappeared, immolated in the small lake of fire that spread across the cobbles, then simmered out. A ghastly reek of charred flesh suffused the air. More of Mustaf's officers were riding roughshod through the mob. They cut out whole companies of men by means of the whips. Beyond the great walls, voices were raised in savage war cries. Those cries, and the threat they signalled, at last made the officer's whips unnecessary.

Most of the men, realizing at last the peril that menaced the city, turned of their own accord toward the dozens of ladders, went clambering up.

The balcony on which Mustaf and Huz al Hussayn had stood remained empty, haunted by flickering shadows cast by another fire-pot burning itself out just below. Dismally Brak realized he had little chance of locating the vizier now. Things were in too chaotic a state. Reluctantly, he turned and shambled toward the outer wall.

At least from the rampart he would be able to keep up on the progress of the battle. Perhaps Mustaf ben Medi would return eventually to see how the fighting fared. At that time, Brak could tell him of his suspicions. To be truthful, Brak suspected the vizier would dismiss his tale as idle supposition. Huz would certainly deny it vehemently. His advancement depended upon his being the savior of the city. Besides, Brak felt certain that the wily Ilona had never revealed to Huz that she served the Gords, or even hinted thus.

Waiting his turn at the base of the ladder, Brak pondered on how Ilona might have come to the city. Shipwrecked like himself, had she been cast ashore? Or had she rejoined her own people first, and only later infiltrated Rodar's kingdom to menace it from within? Either way, her arrival had been disastrous.

Presently Brak's turn came to climb the ladder. He scrambled up. One of Mustaf's officers waited at the top, bawling instructions. More fire-pots flashed through the night sky. The Gord artillery officers had not quite got the range as yet. For every ball of flame which landed within the square, half a dozen fell short.

Brak joined a long chain of men passing heavy stones up

one ladder and along the rampart to a pitifully small rock-caster, one of four ramshackle siege machines on view along the platform. Even as he labored, tossing the heavy stones to the next man in line, Brak stared in fascination at the scene revealed on the plain below the walls.

The Gord army—it looked several thousand strong—had advanced to well within a half-league of the mighty rampart. Torches by the hundreds winked around the numerous heavy siege engines casting fire-pots and mighty boulders which began to batter at the walls. Each time one of the latter struck, the platforms swayed, and faint creakings shook the wall's foundation.

The staff of a great banner was planted at the forefront of the Gord force. The banner itself was roped and pegged at the corners. A gigantic image of the horned goat-god of the Gords, lit by reflection from torches, leered at the defenders.

Drawn up behind the enemy siege engines and the en-camped foot soldiers were the scythe-chariots, row upon row of blade-wheeled juggernauts. The helmet-plumes of their drivers danced in the wind. Their blades glinted blue. The chariots were of no use in such a siege, Brak realized. But should the walls be breached, as the Gords were attempting to breach them now with the flying boulders, then the scythe-chariots could sweep in unopposed. This thought seemed to be in everyone's mind, including that of an officer who rushed down the line:

"Pass the rocks quickly, citizens! If the Gords once pene-trate the walls, those chariots will be impossible to stop. They will thunder to the holy of holies, claim the Sacred Lamb Fleece and hand us defeat before we have begun to oppose them! If ever they capture the Fleece, we're finished. So bend your backs to it, men! Pass the rocks faster!"

Actually the officer's pleas were futile. Already the softer citizens pressed into service were showing signs of flagging. Men fainted or reeled away, retching, not accustomed to the labors of war. Even the officers' whips could not drive them back. Brak felt a vast sense of weariness, futility creep into his bones.

Some dark conspiracy was afoot. It involved Huz and Ilona, he knew. He foresaw unguessable destruction coming soon. What form it would take, he could not say. But he had seen enough of Ilona's power to know that the citizens of Rodar's city-state would not be prepared to counter it.

The rock-casters of the Gords worked with meticulous precision, slamming the walls with telling regularity once the artillerists found the proper range. Tremor after tremor shook the ramparts. The night wore on in a kind of delirium.

Soon Brak's hands were blistered and raw from tossing the heavy stones passed up the ladders from large carts coming and going in the square below. Gradually the stars began to pale. False dawn approached. The bombardment of the Gords did not slacken. Indeed, it grew more intense.

Officers passed a ration of sour wine to the defenders. The taste of it did little to rouse Brak's flagging spirits. As the soldier carrying the fat wineskin was passing down the line, Brak called out:

"Soldier? It is important that I speak with the vizier. Can one of your officers locate him?"

The soldier was in short temper: "It is more important that you stay at your post, clod. Unless, of course, you wish to perish by letting the Gords conquer. As for Mustaf—" The soldier spat. "—his whereabouts are unknown. Probably he's huddled under silk coverlets, surrounded by a thousand troops in his bedchamber. Back to work!"

The big barbarian had no further opportunity to argue. Covered with soot and sweat, he returned to the task of passing the stones. Perhaps he should slip away from the ramparts to the house of Phonicios. In the event the siege was successful, the merchant who had befriended him might need his sword-arm to defend his very doorstep.

As Brak was mulling this question, a new shout of alarm rose from the ramparts, followed by a mighty crash. The entire platform shook violently.

"The wall is breached!" someone shrieked. "Jaal preserve us, the wall is in ruins!"

Work stopped entirely. Men clung precariously to their perches. Below and to the right, a sizeable amount of rubble lay at the foot of a fresh hole in the wall. Above the boulder-sized opening, a fissure appeared. Rapidly it widened, spread upward.

Men fled from the platform just above, too late. The crack reached the top of the wall. The platform shivered and snapped in half.

Citizens caught on either of the broken ends tumbled into space, fell screaming to their death on the rubble-heap below. All around Brak, men began to curse and mumble fearfully to themselves. Out on the plain, the scythe-chariots had moved forward in tight ranks, preparing to enter the city. Already several companies of Gord foot-soldiers had rushed to the breach. A few penetrated and were engaged in bloody combat.

At last the defenders succeeded in blocking off the flow of Gords through the shattered wall. Engineer companies rushed up with carts full of boulders, which they heaped in front of the breach. But other cracks were appearing in the wall now. And the thundering pound of the enemy siege-rocks remained steady. All of the defense platforms began to sag visibly. Several sections were hastily evacuated.

Exhausted beyond exhaustion, Brak the barbarian threw a stone to the hands of his neighbor in the human supply line. Then another. Another. Blood from broken blisters trickled down his wrists. The sky lightened. Warhorns sounded on the plain. Gord soldiers unpegged the ropes holding down the god-banner, readying to move it forward. Where, thought Brak, was Mustaf's mighty weapon of magic that could stem the impending defeat?

Now Brak began to doubt that Huz had done anything more than promise aid to Mustaf ben Medi. Probably the vizier had already taken ship from the port, abandoning his people to a fruitless struggle in which they would be slaughtered.

The platform lurched, creaked. One greybeard beside Brak pawed at the air. Vainly Brak grabbed for him. He was a fraction slow. The old man slipped over the edge shrieking. He struck the cobbles of the square with a bone-mashing thud, just as an officer nearby cried:

"Evacuate the walls! Down the ladders! Hurry! *The wall's breached below us—!*"

Brak joined the mad exodus, reaching the bottom and leaping away just as another Gord missile came sailing through the weakened wall. In a cloud of stinging pumice, the platform overhead gave way. The last unlucky defenders half way down the ladders fell the rest of the way, pulped to red slime beneath whole sections of the wall which sheared off like rotten wood.

Brak narrowly missed being caught under the fall of debris. Now he stood with his hand across his brow to shield his eyes against the increasing glare of the sun. A voice broke out high and keening:

"Jaal! Jaal! *Aieeeeeeee—!*"

The person who had screamed was a burly officer up on one of the still-solid sections of the platform. The officer pointed back toward the center of the city. His hand trembled and his mouth hung slack. He dropped to his knees and began to sway back and forth, foaming at the mouth, biting his own lips in madness.

Brak swung around. So did a thousand others, a thousand more. A shadow fell across the square—

Smash.

Beneath Brak's naked feet, the cobbles rocked and shuddered.

Smash.

The earth trembled again.

Smash.

Brak pressed his palms against his naked flanks, digging his nails in. The pain told him that he was not mad.

All around rose wailing, cursing, moaning. Brak's neck ached because his head was thrown back to look at what had cast the shadow.

Smash.

The bronze foot came down again. Buildings swayed.

Smash.

Men tore at their clothing, their flesh, convinced that the final holocaust was upon them.

Smash.

Great cracks radiated out in the paving each time the bronze foot came down.

Gilded with sun-shafts that shone over the rooftops, a giant came striding along one of the broad avenues which led to the walls from the city's heart. Its shadow fell ten blocks ahead of it. It was the mighty bronze statue of Jaal the Leveller, twenty times as tall as a man, and its huge head was turning, and its cyclops eye shone nearly as bright as the sun itself as it walked.

Smash, smash, smash.

The buildings between which the idol walked were as toys by comparison to its size. With each step the incredible colossus started the earth a-trembling. From the various buildings men and women leaned out to glimpse the walking nightmare. The idol was perhaps five squares distant now, its shadow engulfing hundreds of men huddled together in the main square, around Brak.

Smash, smash, smash.

Onward it came, great bronze-scaly arms swinging, great bronze legs lifting. Along its route men and women driven out of their minds by the sight hurled themselves from windows in suicidal frenzy. Brak's mind throbbed with disbelief as the colossus kept coming, hugely real.

"Run!" men were crying. "Save yourselves! Jaal the Leveller has turned against us!"

At once the defenders around Brak began to flee. They scattered across the shadowed square as the idol continued its march.

More shouts rose from those nearest the point where the avenue opened onto the square:

"Hold! Don't be afraid! Look, the vizier is coming— leading the giant!"

Here and there, frightened souls continued their headlong plunge into doorways around the square. Most, however, stopped. Brak went loping toward the square's opposite side. He'd caught a glimpse of a burnished chariot. As he joined the press pushing nearer to the avenue, he saw runners ahead of the chariot, which was drawn by three matched ebony warhorses.

Within the chariot rode Mustaf ben Medi. Beside him, smiling, preening-proud and splendidly-attired, was Huz al Hussayn.

Smash, smash, smash.

The idol continued its march down the avenue, a square to the rear of the chariot. Mustaf had his hands raised, palms downward. He was shouting to the people in the buildings along the route, attempting to quiet them. But the frightened dwellers in the buildings paid more attention to the idol than to Mustaf and Huz.

The vizier signalled for the chariot to halt. The runners caught the bridles of the warhorses, brought them pawing to a stop. Mustaf consulted with Huz al Hussayn. The latter nodded, turned in the chariot. With a theatrical flourish, he made a gesture to the gigantic idol.

Its left foot came down, *smash*, rocking the earth. The foot did not move again.

*   *   *

Bronze cast back the sun's rays. The colossus stood immobile, head inclined downward. Its huge cyclopean eye pulsed with pearly white radiance, the only sign that it lived.

From windows closest to the chariot, feeble cheers went up, followed by shrieks of joy. All at once the temper of the crowd changed. Beaming, Mustaf signalled the runners. The chariot lurched forward.

A lane opened across the square. Through this the chariot rolled. The idol began to walk again, pulverizing the pavement with each step. People near Brak pressed ahead, anxious to witness the passing of the marvel, yet trembling too as the huge shadow flickered over them.

Brak's neck ached violently from craning upward. A nagging fear worried the edge of his mind. Mustaf and Huz had calmed the crowds by showing that the bronze colossus was under their control. Yet Brak was certain that The Thief-Taker's spirit must be activating the monster. That meant the idol was actually under Ilona's guidance, wherever she was. Huz did not possess the skills of sorcery to work the feat.

Unless, of course, Brak thought suddenly, Huz had killed the witch after wresting her secrets from her.

As the idol lumbered past, making Brak's teeth rattle every time it stepped, the big barbarian felt a rush of relief. That must be it! Ilona was dead! Perhaps this was one time when Huz's duplicity boded good, rather than evil.

The Jaal statue slowed as it approached the wall. It stopped again, swinging its monstrous one-eyed head to encompass the entire horizon. People shoved up beside its great bronze feet, to whisper and to marvel.

The city wall barely reached to the idol's middle. From the plain outside, cries of consternation and horror from the entire Gord army could be heard. A jubilant officer on one of the remaining sections of platform cupped his hands around his mouth, bawled down:

"The Gord chariots are turning! The goat-god banner is struck! The Gords run—*in terror!*"

Still the idol stood peering over the wall like some grotesque, brainless child of gigantic size. Near its feet, people began an impromptu dance, cheering hysterically. In their chariot Huz and Mustaf smiled at one another, accepting the plaudits of the crowd. A scene of desolation only moments ago, the square now rang with victory-cries, laughter, wild relieved sobs. Soldiers slapped one another's backs. Men capered, made coarse jokes about the cowardice of the Gords.

In the midst of all this confusion, no one was prepared for the sudden movement of the statue.

A few people clustered at its feet sensed a change. They looked up curiously. The white fire in the idol's eye was pulsing—

Without warning, its mighty bronze foot lifted above the heads of the crowd. The foot came down—

Smash.

Jaal the Leveller stamped on three dozen citizens and more, crushing them all.

Fresh panic broke out around the idol's feet, where the cobbles ran with rivers of blood squirting from the corpses of the victims. The idol lifted both its bronze hands. It formed them into fists.

With two blows it smashed the high city wall to bits.

Shrieking and cursing at each other, Mustaf and Huz struggled with the traces of their chariot. The horses pawed the air and neighed in terror. Jaal reached out, grasped two sections of the wall still standing, shook them. The entire structure from one edge of the square to the other began to shudder and crack.

A moment later, avalanches of rock and rubble fell inward upon the hapless thousands clustered in the wall's shadow.

Nearer the avenue than the wall, Brak found himself buffeted, nearly upset by the cattlelike stampeding of the terror-maddened people. Through the dust rising from the shattered ramparts, Brak heard war-horns blast again. A shout echoed from many throats. All around, hands pointed upward.

Brak's belly wrenched as he glanced that way. On one of the highest rooftops overlooking the square stood a slender girl, pale-robed, arms outstretched toward the idol. Her blonde yet gray-streaked hair blew in the wind.

"*Ilona,*" Brak breathed.

Abruptly, he was shoved, hurled along in the sudden flight of people down the avenue toward the heart of the city. He fought free of the running mob, flattened against the wall of a building. He watched the holocaust in the square as the luckless ones who did not run swiftly enough were pulped under the feet of Jaal when the idol turned full around and began to march into the city again.

Smash, smash, smash.

Beyond the shattered ramparts now reduced to ground level in most places, there were whirling reflections, blue-bright, metallic. The scythe-machines of the Gords began to roll.

The Gord commanders had recognized Ilona on the rooftop. The columns of chariots swept toward the defenseless square. As the wheels turned behind the plunging horses, the whirling blades mowed down every bit of brush and weed on the plain, as they would shortly mow down a human harvest.

A more familiar chariot flashed, gleamed and vanished in shadows down a side street. Mustaf ben Medi and Huz—Huz whose self interest had betrayed an entire city—had managed to escape.

Brak remained pressed against the building as Jaal reached the mid-point in the square. *Smash, smash, smash.* At each step, hundreds more perished under his bronze feet.

The people fleeing past Brak were like wild beasts. All around, he heard senseless screaming, prayers, cries of, "To the temple of the Sacred Lamb Fleece! The gods will protect us there!"

The Jaal-statue was marching toward the avenue now,

driving the frightened thousands before it. Across the way, Brak saw several people flee into doorways, obviously hoping for sanctuary on the rooftops. Wheeling, Brak ducked into a similar door.

He climbed several flights of sour stairs. He emerged on the sunlit roof overlooking the city. The buildings were close-packed in this quarter. Their upper stories nearly touched. People were utilizing this escape route. But Jaal did not spare them.

On the street's opposite side, the idol reached out as it passed. With one sweep of its fist it demolished an entire row of six structures, sending buildings and human wreckage tumbling in one awful cloud.

But the building on whose roof Brak had taken refuge survived. Jaal passed it by. Thus Brak the barbarian saw the final horror of all—the huge idol somehow scooped up its mistress.

Hair streaming like gold in the wind, Ilona stood on the idol's right shoulder. She clung to its bronze ear as it marched ahead through a field of corpses. Her head was thrown back, red-mouthed. Though her voice could not be heard above the noise of Jaal's footsteps and crashing buildings, Brak could see that she was shrieking with triumphant laughter.

Behind, in the square, the first of the Gord scythe-chariots rolled in.

Chapter XI

AFTERWARD, BRAK THE barbarian was unable to tell a coherent story of how he managed to reach the central square of Rodar's city. But reach it he did, via the rooftops, along with thousands of others.

What he remembered of it was nothing more than a series of fragmentary, nightmarish impressions—

Jaal's monstrous bronze-cast head swaying past the building on which Brak had taken cover.

Ilona's hair like a yellow-gray banner.

The Gord chariots in the streets below, hub to hub, moving rapidly, six ranks to a squadron, four chariots to a rank, harvesting the stragglers. Whirling blades spat back shards of silvery sunlight, sprayed great curtains of blood against the walls of buildings as scores of Rodar's people were caught by the blades and mutilated piecemeal.

Brak recalled watching the idol turn aside, go lurching and stumbling into another quarter of the city. There, the armories were located. Over the rooftops, its great torso and

destructive hands were visible, the speck of Ilona still clinging to its shoulder.

Brak recalled a wide gulf between rooftops. He leaped it
somehow. He also recalled the pitiful wails and screams of
those whose strength was not sufficient to carry them across.

He followed the human river flowing off the rooftops and
down through labyrinthine passages in some spacious building. He spilled out with the hundreds, the thousands into the
sprawling central plaza before the vast, gracefully-columned
Temple of the Sacred Lamb Fleece.

To the westward, above the tallest buildings, Jaal the
Leveller could be seen, his lower body hidden in a cloud of
dust from the wreckage of the structures he pulverized in his
path. The noise of the idol's march had become so familiar
that Brak all but forgot it as he ran this way, that. Somewhere
in the square he hoped to find the people to whom he owed his
last loyalty when the final battle came.

He was certain the battle would be at hand soon. Jaal's
turning aside was only a temporary diversion. Ilona had
directed the monster into the area where the army's weapons
were stored. Even now, the gigantic idol could be seen
turning, smashing a path back toward the central square.

Terrified crowds flowed up the steps of the Lamb Fleece
temple. Plunging through the mob, Brak saw only unfamiliar
faces, and the wreckage of the altar at the side of the square
where the great idol of Jaal had formerly stood. Across the
way, the equally tall statue of the goddess Ashtir stared
helplessly down on the rioting thousands around her wheeled
feet. The fleeing people cursed her, threw rocks at her base as
they passed, for she had failed them.

Brak struggled into the temple. The crush was unbelievable.
Time and again he was smacked or shoved against a pillar.
He was forced to extricate himself by using his fists and
kicking savagely. Despite the best efforts of the acolytes who
guarded the holy of holies, its teakwood gates had been torn

from their bronze hinges. The inner sanctuary, a cool, pale chamber where beams of sun drifted down, was thronged wall to wall.

There, above another immense altar, a scrap of something hung from a thick ring of solid gold. The ṛng was supported on two tall, intricately carved pillars. A bar of sunlight struck part of the fleece which hung from the ring. The fleece was revealed to be gray, ancient, even moth-eaten. But in front of this sacred relic hundreds were kneeling, saying their final death-prayers.

A balcony ran around the entire chamber. On all sides of it, groups of soldiers and acolytes watched the scene of panic below. Far across the room, Brak espied a thatch of reddish hair.

Stumbling, staggering, panting, he fought his way through the kneeling supplicants while screaming, pandemonium, roars and crashes of destruction echoed from without.

"Calix! Phonicios!" Brak shouted.

The reddish head turned. Brak saw familiar blue eyes. Then saw another stocky figure with a gray shot beard. In moments, he was surrounded by Phonicios's householders. Like most everyone else in the city, they had sought the refuge of the temple.

Phonicios's face was wan with fright as he clapped Brak's arm feebly. "Barbarian! We thought you dead at the gates."

"Nearly," Brak replied, dizzy with weariness. Calix braced him up. Brak noticed Saria standing beside the freedman, head bowed in prayer. "At least we can stand together if the end comes," he finished.

"Do not say that!" Phonicios exclaimed. "Surely Mustaf will be able to halt the bronze monster."

"Nothing can stop it," Brak returned. "Ilona controls it. Gods! If a sword would avail against it, I'd give my life. So would a thousand others here, I'll wager. But nothing can stand against a god of bronze."

Saria's gentle eyes gleamed, wet with sorrow. "This never was your quarrel, Brak."

"Perhaps not at the start," he answered. "Yet it became mine. The least I can do is await the end of it like a man, among the people who befriended me." One of Brak's brawny hands lifted to the kneeling hundreds all around. "If I knew the prayers they're saying, I would even join in."

Phonicios was about to speak when suddenly, from outside, more rioting thousands attempted to press into the already close-packed temple.

"Jaal!" they cried. "Jaal nears the square!"

Smash, smash, smash.

The screams rose into the sunbeams drifting into the chamber. The floor trembled.

"Kneel, daughter!" Phonicios dropped to his knees. "And you, Calix, my good steward. Let us pray together, that our death from the gods will be swift and—" Phonicios cried out in alarm as, directly ahead of him, a citizen pitched forward, kicking and writhing.

From the man's back protruded an arrow whose quills still quivered.

Brak realized that the arrow had been aimed at Phonicios's back. Only the merchant's kneeling had prevented a hit. Fresh shouting broke out. Heads lifted. Brak whirled.

"It's Huz," Calix whispered, eyes round as blue stones. "And he—*Saria!*"

Another arrow came bolting down from the balcony. Huz was crouched just behind and to one side of the great ring which held the Sacred Lamb Fleece. Brak heard Saria cry out, saw her sag. The arrow stuck from her right shoulder.

Menacing the people on the balcony with his freshly-nocked bow, Huz bawled down in the sudden silence:

"Stand aside, cattle! It's Phonicios I came here to finish— Phonicios, the hypocritical pig who has caused me all this calamity."

*   *   *

Huz's eyes were glazed, maniacal. He drew back the bow-string. Along the balcony, soldiers were running at the crazed merchants from both directions. Bedraggled, his greasy hair flying, Huz spun around, saw them, released the bowstring. The arrow sank into the throat of the first soldier on his right. The man pitched back.

The soldiers racing in from the other side hesitated. Their commander cried, "Move forward, you cowards! Seize him! He is the one who fled from the vizier's chariot! The one responsible for betraying us—for loosing Jaal!"

When the crowd heard this, they had a ready target for their hate. They began to shriek filthy epithets and wave their fists. On the balcony, Huz looked deranged, his mind cracked by all the misfortunes which had befallen him. He drew back a step, swinging his bow one way, then another.

Still the soldiers hesitated. There was little to be gained by capturing a madman when they would all die soon enough.

Smash, smash, smash.

The temple rocked. Outside, the screaming was continuous, ear-deadening. A red curtain of fury dropped over Brak's mind, blinding him to reason. It wiped out his weariness and his knowledge of the futility of revenge. That armor-clad, scraggle-bearded apparition capering on the balcony was the person who had released havoc upon the city—

Leaping across the fallen Saria whose eyes were closed and whose gown bloomed with an ominous flower of blood around the shaft of the up-thrusting arrow, Brak began to run.

He kicked aside any who got in his way. Straight to the base of the twin pillars he charged. Two captains in armor barred his path. Snarling, growling like a beast, Brak bowled them over. From the scabbard of one he pulled the man's shimmering broadsword.

He clamped the dull edge of the great weapon between his teeth. He leaped high. Monkeylike, he began to climb one of the pillars, using its flutings and carvings for foot- and hand-holds.

He raced upward with surprising speed. His muscles ached, tormented by the effort. But the sudden dam-burst of hate within him lent him new strength.

Above, the golden ring with the mothy fleece hanging from it blazed in sunlight, framed by the ring. Huz leaned from the balcony, bow bent. Brak kept climbing.

The arrow sang from the bow. It glanced from the haft end of the sword Brak clenched in his teeth. The arrow went skittering over the heads of the crowd. People wailed. Brak's left hand slipped.

He nearly plunged off the pillar. His fingers, gripping a carved animal-snout, nearly broke until he was able to take hold with his other hand and, bracing his feet, continue his swift climb.

Huz's face was a phantasm, seeming to float in the sunlight framed by the great gold ring. Brak was nearly to the top of the pillar. Armor flashed. The soldiers, spurred by Brak's determination, charged in.

Huz shot another arrow out of the quiver on his shoulder. The soldier nearest him pitched forward on his face. Huz disappeared.

Brak threw his left hand high, grasped the bottom of the gold ring, which was thick as a man's arm. Abruptly Huz came into sight again. He moved with the swiftness of one in whom madness had produced exceeding strength. Huz's blade licked out, darted down toward the ring as he leaned far over the balcony rail.

Hanging from the ring by both hands, Brak dangled in space, helpless if Huz were to hack at his gripping fingers—

Instead, Huz's sword-point snaked under the edge of the Sacred Lamb Fleece. Huz's hand twitched. The Fleece was jerked upward through the air by the point of the sword.

An instant later Brak clambered up hand over hand, stood swaying inside the gold ring. Huz had raced away from the

balcony edge, the Fleece in his grasp. His arrow and quiver lay discarded.

Fresh moanings and sobbings rose from the packed temple floor. Even as Brak swung his weight to get the gold ring moving—now further away from the balcony, now closer—he understood dimly what Huz planned. He had snared the Fleece in desperation. He intended to rush out to the Gords, turn the relic over to them and thus give them the victory. In return, no doubt he would expect his own life to be spared.

The ring swung far out from the balcony, paused, swung inward—and Brak leaped.

His hands groped for the balcony rail as he flew through the air. With one hand, he missed. His other found purchase. In an instant he was over the rail and racing for a staircase where confused, befuddled soldiers were attempting to pursue the vanished Huz.

Smash, smash, smash.

The very temple walls rocked as Jaal drew nearer the central square. Up the staircase Brak raced, two risers at a time. He bowled soldiers aside in twos and threes. Several called for him to halt, but only feebly. He was a fearsome sight. His great body was hacked and scarred by recent wounds. His long braid flew. There was a glare of rage in his eyes.

Presently Brak was alone on the spiral stone stair, racing upward and upward, around and around. He jerked to a halt, mighty chest heaving. Breath raced hard in and out of his lungs.

From the clamor of voices and the continual rocking, grinding, thudding which signalled the approach of the witch-driven Jaal, Brak sorted out another sound. It was lighter, more rapid than the others.

The sound of sandals whacking stone as their owner fled. Huz!

Leaping forward again, Brak soon reached the top of the staircase. Sunlight blazed. He plunged past an ornamental lattice-work doorway standing ajar at the top. He pulled up short.

The wind blew briskly, whipping out the tail of the lion-pelt at his waist. On every side, smoke-palls rose into heaven. Brak could see the entire city from the temple roof. Nearly half the buildings were in ruins. Far below, in count-less streets, the scythe-chariot blades whirled and flashed with light.

The central square was still packed from edge to edge with thousands of persons. All struggled to enter the temple. Scarcely three squares away, marching stolidly forward, kicking out with bronze hands and bronze feet to demolish now this structure, now that one, came Jaal. A yellow banner marked the presence of Ilona riding on his shoulder.

"Huz?" Brak shouted. His voice was ragged, near to cracking. "Merchant?"

The sunny wind, so incongruous against the panorama of destruction spread out on every hand, bore Brak's words away. Cautiously Brak stepped forward. His spine prickled.

One more pace and he was free of shadow cast by the little cupola on the temple roof. He had emerged through the door set in one side of the cupola. The roof of the temple was high-railed, tiled with smooth mosaics, fitted here and there with marble benches. Nothing stirred, except the wind.

Brak turned his head slightly. The maddened merchant must be hiding directly behind the cupola, Brak reasoned. There was no other place of concealment.

Despite the coolness of the air, chill sweat began to race down Brak's chest. Slowly, slowly, he pivoted on his naked feet. Now he faced the cupola again. On each side it was nearly twice as wide as a man's body, affording good protec-tion for a hidden assassin. Brak licked his lips.

Huz knew he was being pursued. He would doubtless anticipate the barbarian lunging either to the left or right, around the cupola.

Trying to ignore the mind-deadening bea.
bronze feet crushing everything before it, Brak studi
height of the cupola roof.

He squatted down, hoping for the strength he needed, and
the luck. The cupola was but a scant bit higher than his own
head. Gazing up at it, Brak wrapped his fingers more tightly
about the broadsword haft. He sprang.

In mid-air he kicked with his brawny legs. He seized the
cupola's edge with his free hand, pulled himself up. Over and
over he went rolling, slowing just in time to jump erect before
he toppled off the other side.

In the split instant which it took him to gain his feet on the
cupola roof, he saw a flash of ebony and armor directly
below. Huz was crouched in the shadow of the cupola wall,
ceremonial sword drawn from the gilt scabbard Mustaf must
have provided him in the hour when Huz stood triumphant
before the vizier, the benefactor of all the city.

Huz spun around. He gave a flick to his left arm. The
Sacred Lamb Fleece dropped to the tiles. Huz brought his
curved blade whipping around in an arc just above eye level,
aiming for Brak's naked legs braced on the cupola roof.

Like some sort of savage ceremonial dancer, Brak let out a
shrill, wordless scream of rage and jumped up, lifting both
feet off the cupola. The blade slashed by. Brak's feet
slammed the roof as he came down. He bent his knees,
straightened them, propelled himself forward through the
air. As he fell, he whipped his sword around toward Huz's
neck.

The disgraced merchant quickly darted out of the way.
Brak scrambled up. The two enemies circled one another.
Huz's fine trappings were begrimed, torn in many places.
The ornate gold circlet which had replaced the scrap of rag to
bind up his long black hair had slipped. As a result, strands of
greasy dark hair blew around Huz's cheeks like the snaky
tendrils of a medusa. Huz's long nails seemed to twitch an

bend as he grasped his swordhandle tighter, crouching, circling, circling—

Brak circled too. In Huz's eyes was complete unreason. Dollops of spittle hung and gleamed in the hairs of the beard on his chin.

"Slut spawn!" Huz breathed, teeth ugly yellow in the sunlight. "Dung man! Until you came, Phonicios was helpless. 'Tis you I owe death more than the swine from the Guild."

Cautiously, cautiously, their feet shuffling in rhythm, the two men moved round and round.

Their eyes never left one another. Each waited for the other to make the fateful lunge.

Brak's voice was a hardly human growl: "Merchant, your mind has betrayed you. For you owe me not a whit. It is the people of this city who owe you, merchant. Owe you a dying ten times worse than any dying ever known before. Look, merchant. Look down at the square. Look out yonder in the streets, where the dead lie by the scores. The dead cry for payment, merchant. It was you who loosed that bronze giant on them. You who let Ilona gull you into believing she was an ally."

"I did not know she served the Gords!" Huz shrieked wildly. "When I found her sitting in a tavern, she said she came from a far land, had been a prisoner of the Gord admiral, had been cast up on the shore in the aftermath of the sea battle—" His voice keened higher. "I only used her to take back what Phonicios took from me. *I did not know!*"

"Phonicios never stole your life," Brak growled. "You have stolen thousands in return."

"I'll steal yours before I'm finished, dung-man!" Huz cried, feinting suddenly to the left.

Brak readied his guard. Huz cackled, whipped around on his right toe, came charging across the roof straight at Brak.

Because of the tremendous exertions his mighty frame had endured the past hours, Brak's responses were a fraction slow. He jerked back on his right foot, hauled up his broad-sword, having no time to thrust. Huz's curved weapon hacked against the barbarian's sword.

Sparks flew, metal rang. Brak heaved. Huz danced backward, off balance. He capered a moment, arms waving wildly.

Brak dodged in for the killing stroke. He had misjudged. Huz's flailing sword-arm chopped the air near Brak's own arm. His blade dug into Brak's bicep, sliced free.

The big barbarian nearly doubled over with the exquisite agony of the thin steel sliding in and sliding out of his muscle. He managed to stay on his feet by sheer will.

Huz pressed his advantage, tittering. His eyes were no more than glazed stones now, staring demonically out of his head. While Brak swayed, struggling to remain on his feet, Huz came gliding in under his guard.

The big barbarian turned, hacked downward. His blade missed Huz's arm, caught his sword. Instantly Huz whipped his steel back from the contact. He hurled his right arm to the rear until it was stretched to its limit. Then he slashed it forward again, sword-blade a horizontal flash of white brilliance in the sunlight.

At that moment, Brak's brain clouded. His knees unlocked. He keeled onto his face, slamming hard on the mosaics. Huz's swath missed.

Brak flopped over onto his spine. Short cape fluttering, Huz scuttled in close, leaned over, grinning as he drove his blade downward toward Brak's heart—

Two things Brak did then. Small, desperate things.

He kicked out with his right foot, catching Huz's shin.

And at the same time he lifted his right wrist; lifted it though it weighed heavier than all the silver ingots in the universe.

His broadsword's point stood straight up just as his kick sent Huz off balance, spilled him over. The merchant's mouth flew open. He fell straight onto Brak's blade. The point entered his throat just behind the jawbone and finally jarred, scraping, on the back of the skull.

Huz al Hussayn hung there. The curved sword dropped from his fingers. His legs kicked, thrashed. With his head impaled yet still alive, he stared downward at Brak. His eyes flashed a final horrific disbelief. His tongue shot out, purpling. And, like a boar on a spit, he died.

Groaning, Brak rolled to one side. He let go of the broadsword.

With the great weapon still projecting from his throat, Huz slumped on the tiles. Brak lay a moment, panting and blinking in the sun.

Warm stuff leaked down his arm. Gradually, sounds penetrated into his pain-thumping mind: the cries of the citizens trapped in the square below; the crash of falling buildings; the grinding noise each time Jaal took a step.

Awkwardly, Brak climbed to his feet. He was near to retching. He bent down, tore a long length of material from Huz's cloak. He staggered against the cupola, leaned there. He wound the black stuff around and around his upper arm, pulling it so tight his face contorted in agony and his teeth were bared.

At last, however, the knot was firm. The flow of blood from the long wound was temporarily stanched.

Brak wiped his eyes. He shambled around the cupola, retrieved the Sacred Lamb Fleece and tottered toward the roof rail. Perhaps if he showed the ancient relic to the crowds below, they would take heart.

He stumbled against the rail, the Fleece flapping in the wind. Across the square, the Jaal idol had paused. Its monstrous eye surveyed the thousands rioting in panic at its feet. That cyclopean eye burned ten times whiter-hot than the sun. And Ilona's hair streamed out as she rode the statue's shoulder.

Brak could imagine her mocking smile of victory as she watched the masses waiting to be trampled under the idol's feet. With a weak grimace, Brak peered down at the mothy relic over his arm.

Idiocy to show it to the people.

Idiocy to fight any longer.

The day had been lost.

In a moment more, Jaal the Leveller would begin to walk toward the temple. The finis would be written to the history of the city-state of Rodar, Prince of the Two Bays.

Weakened, full of this sense of defeat, Brak leaned on the rail in the wind, shaking his head.

Then, abruptly, he stiffened.

He laughed.

It was wholly mad. Desperate and unthinkable.

But was it not better than waiting?

At least—he laughed a second time—he could die like a warrior.

Staring intently at the one remaining statue in the square, the bronze image of the begirdled Ashtir, Brak heard a sound. He turned.

Towering to the sky, Jaal was moving again.

Chapter XII

ARM OUTFLUNG, ILONA WAS RIGID on the idol's shoulder. There could be no mistaking where she pointed.

She pointed at Brak.

In the square far below, thousands craned around, stared upward. Ilona's arm rose, snapped downward. Jaal changed direction. His bronze feet crushed several dozen not quick enough to dart back.

The Gord witch had sighted Brak silhouetted against the bright sky, the Sacred Lamb Fleece flung over his arm. Now Jaal the Leveller began to advance toward him, between masses of frantic citizens desperately struggling to stay out of his path. Ilona knew the significance of the Lamb Fleece, and she wanted it.

But Brak was already racing away toward the far side of the temple roof.

He pulled up short at the edge, peered over. Several stories below, a low, curved wing of the temple led around toward the side of the square where the gigantic statue of Ashtir flashed back sunlight from her bronzed flesh. Swallowing hard, Brak jumped up to the rail. He edged over the side and began a long, perilous descent via one of several carved pillars standing out from the temple's side.

Clinging precariously whole stories above the street, Brak was in clear sight of the thousands below. They saw that he had the Sacred Lamb Fleece wrapped around his shoulders, the tag-ends knotted at his throat like a cloak. Confused, alarmed outcries came from their throats.

The wind whipped at Brak. Its force threatened to dislodge his precarious hand-holds. But at last, panting, he reached the roof of the lower temple wing. He set off along it at a run.

Jaal the Leveller had turned in the middle of the square, lumbering after him. Soon Brak dropped down from the wing's roof into a narrow alley-way he had sighted from above. Pelting along this alley in thick shadow, he saw ahead the bronzed backside of the goddess Ashtir. At the statue's base were the great iron-rimmed wood wheels twice as tall as himself. By means of these wheels, he remembered Phonicios saying, the goddess was moved into the fields to bless the crops.

Once more, out in the square, Jaal the Leveller turned. *Smash, smash, smash.* The statue clumped toward the bronze goddess.

The barbarian reached the base of the female statue. He ran around one of the mammoth bronze heels, then the other. Finally he spied the outline of a narrow doorway in the rear surface of the left heel. An ornamental handle responded to his touch. Lamb Fleece flapping, he ducked into the musty, metal-smelling interior of the statue's foot.

Far overhead the hollow idol, light gleamed faintly. Something blackish swayed, outlined against the light. Brak seized with both hands, discovered it was a ladder of rope, leading upward.

Levers and pulleys, Phonicios had said. Levers and pulleys—

Brak was gambling with a city's life.

*   *   *

His mighty body was nearly at point of collapse, but still he managed to climb upward, rung after swaying rung. The light overhead seemed to recede, blur. He knew it was only a trick of his exhausted mind. Rung after rung he clambered, pulling himself at last, nearly spent, onto a crude platform.

The platform projected from the inner surface of Ashtir's face, just below the pupil-less eyes. The wind whistled through those two great eye-openings. The openings were slightly above Brak's head, affording him an oblique view of the sky. He got a terrible start when, suddenly, the head of Jaal, quite close, appeared in the space framed by the left eye. Jaal was moving closer—

In a moment Brak got a clear view of Ilona on Jaal's shoulder. Her face was strained, haggard, as she cried incantations and directions at the spirit-essence somewhere within the idol. Struggling for calm, Brak surveyed the arrangement of ivory-handled levers protruding up through the surface of the control platform.

He put both hands on the central lever. He tugged hard. With a scream of iron tires, the Ashtir idol began to roll forward.

Hastily Brak slammed the lever back in place. He had almost sent the statue thundering directly into Jaal's path.

Two other levers, set at angles on the right and left, offered promise. Brak found the right-hand one hard to move, bent his great back until the muscles stood out like serpents beneath the skin. At last the lever freed.

Somewhere, pulleys whirred, dropped, clanked. Slowly, ponderously, the statue swung to the right.

Fresh frenzied cries broke out from the terrified populace. The Ashtir figure swung completely around. Brak could no longer see Jaal the Leveller.

He hauled back on the right-hand lever. Then he pulled the central one. The Ashtir statue shuddered, rolled forward. Far below, Brak heard a wooden crunching, grinding. Small houses? Sheds near the square? Impossible to tell. Brak only prayed that what he knew about The Thief-Taker was correct, to stay out of the way of the rolling juggernaut which Brak was forced to direct almost blindly. Through the eye openings he could see nothing but the sky now.

While the statue rolled, Brak clambered up in one of the open eyes. He peered down. Ahead, past more small build-ings which the statue was demolishing as it rolled and bumped along, the idol's path would intersect a broad av-enue. Far to the right Brak glimpsed the burnished cobalt of the two bays, with the long mole extending out toward the island which rose to form the pair of channels. Clinging precariously in the wind there in the open right eye of the goddess, Brak waited until the statue had nearly reached the avenue. Then he leaped back inside.

Once more he tugged frantically on the oblique right-hand lever. He heard the pulleys whirr and whine again. Creaking, straining, the goddess-statue swung into the center of the avenue.

Brak drew the middle lever back again. The statue began to roll faster. The street surface inclined down toward the harbor. It was impossible to slacken speed, Brak discovered, because of this slope in the paving.

The wheeled statue gained momentum, a bronze-breasted goddess seeming to float about the housetops.

Smash, smash, smash. Jaal came on, pursuing.

Brak fell across the central lever, laying his sweated cheek against the cool ivory knob. He sobbed with great ragged gasps. The opening gambit had succeeded. It was a sort of gargantuan jest, larger than life: one death-reeking idol lum-bering in pursuit of another.

Yet upon the sex of the statue in which he was clattering swiftly down to the harbor, Brak had banked his final hope for success. He thought he heard Ilona screaming filthy

imprecations at the Jaal-idol. Impossible. No sound could carry that far.

Yet the shuddering and thundering of the earth grew heavier by the moment. *Smash, smash, smash.*

The evil spirit-essence within Jaal had belonged to The Thief-Taker. Brak had gambled upon the essence of that spirit being as Phonicios had described it—lustful.

Now it was following its own lustful bent, if Brak could believe the thundering tremors which jarred even the mighty Ashtir image rolling along toward the harbor dead ahead. Exactly as it had done within a smaller Jaal-idol the night Phonicios's house was attacked, the lustful spirit of The Thief-Taker had gone in pursuit of the one thing which it notoriously craved above all others—a woman. A woman twenty times as high as a human being.

Hanging across the controls, Brak no longer cared what happened to him. If the Jaal-idol would follow the Ashtir statue into the harbor, perhaps the people would have a chance to turn back the invaders. Brak's body shuddered, twitched with each thud of the great wheels as Ashtir rolled over minor obstructions—shattered carts, shop awnings—in the avenue. His mind was darkening.

Smash, smash, smash. Jaal still pursued.

Brak wished that he could see Ilona's face as she rode the idol's shoulder, vainly trying to control the lustful essence of The Thief-Taker. For, a moment ago, between the ponderous thuddings of the bronze idol's feet, Brak had clearly heard sound that was not imagination. Above the wind, foul curses came drifting through the open eye-windows. Brak recognized Ilona's voice, screaming helplessly.

A purplish hand, seven-fingered, tickled Brak's forearm.

Goggling, he jerked back from the control lever.

Out of nothing, a fanged imp materialized.

The imp gibbered, whirling around the chamber inside the great bronze head.

Brak leaped back. He nearly pitched off the edge of the platform to fall down through the hollow statue.

Waving its seven-clawed hands, the imp spun around and round Brak's head, plucking at his face. A mad chittering filled the chamber.

Tired beyond all tiredness, Brak cursed and batted at the thing. His arm passed through it, stinging horribly at the contact.

Out of the floor came twisting a cobalt serpent, coil upon moistly shining coil.

The serpent twitched toward Brak's legs.

A huge, disembodied human eye rocketed toward Brak's head. The eye wept blood-drops at which Brak tried to strike.

A voice rang in his ears. Then another. Then a dozen—cheeping, chittering, growling, moaning, sobbing.

A female corpse wrapped in white shrouds wrapped itself around him, laughing at him, teeth falling out, skin peeling away until only a skull grinned—

The air in the chamber grew black.

Scaly hands, distorted human shapes with obscene configurations whirled round and round Brak's head.

The big barbarian began to laugh hysterically as he batted at the things he could not seize.

Again he struck at air, again. He felt the clammy touch of the things yet he was unable to grapple with them.

A gryphon breathing fire opened its jaws, big as all the chamber, to swallow him. Brak stared into the flames that danced in its maw.

Dimly he remembered a sea-fight, magical creatures upon the water.

Not real! his brain cried.

This is Ilona's final trick. Mind-devils to drive you mad. You cannot fight them with your hands, only with your brain.

They are not real!
They are shadow!
They cannot harm you—

A saber-tooth slid across the chamber floor, chomping at Brak's legs with its wet-dripping fangs.

Brak shouted and hurled himself against the chamber wall, shuddering, quaking, feeling his senses slip away.

In the midst of the welter of nightmare shapes materializing and vanishing all around, in the midst of the cacophony of weird shrieks, screams and laughter, Brak heard another sound. A distant, tinkling voice, calling:

"Barbarian? Barbarian? One way or another, my own power will destroy you. Barbarian? You are done—"

A gargoyle bit his belly.

A fifty-legged spider crawled down his spine.

A vulture with a tiny child's face pecked at his eyes.

Brak held his temples, shrieked unable to control himself.

A last, lost murmur in his brain called out, *They are not real! They cannot harm you—*

Suddenly, knowing he must resist or perish, Brak stood stock still in the center of the rocking chamber, just as the most horrific horror of all, an immense octopus-like thing with a thousand evil black-wet mouths along its tentacles, spun out of nowhere.

The monster enfolded him, prickling his skin, sending blazing bolts of mad, unaccountable terror through his skull—

Brak threw his arms wide like a man crucified.

His back strained.

His temple-veins stood out full of blood and near to bursting.

"Begone!" he screamed. *"Begone, nightmares!"*

"Real, real!" a voice wailed in his mind or elsewhere. "They will *kill* you—"

"Begone, nightmares!"

Brak's throat was raw, bloodraw, crying it. He closed his eyes, hung his head back, dug his nails into his palms until blood ran.

With every last resource of courage in his mighty body strained to the ultimate, he roared like thunder:

"BEGONE!"

Simultaneously, the shapes popped, hissed, burned away, melted, leaving only stench.

And the great wheeled Ashtir statue gave a sickening lurch, dropping—

Brak was tumbled clear across the chamber. For a moment the immense head seemed to tilt forward, the whole statue swaying, tipping dangerously.

Distantly, water splashed, churned. Gasping, Brak crawled up into the open eye, hung there. Cold sweat turned the Sacred Lamb Fleece around his shoulders to a sodden cloak.

The Ashtir statue had lurched out to the end of the mole and dropped the short distance into the harbor. The great wheels still churned, though more slowly now, along the sloping rocky bottom. The surface of the water far below was foamed into immense waves which the Ashtir statue could not be causing. Brak clung in the eye, heard a grinding sound again. Suddenly the frightening shape of Jaal the Leveller lumbered into sight to the left of the Ashtir statue, whose huge wheels were spinning now, immobilized in the muck of the harbor bottom.

On Jaal's shoulder Ilona hung, tearing at her gown, her hair. She pounded her fists against the idol's bronze neck, a picture of demented panic.

Slowly the mighty bronze arms of Jaal the Leveller rose, stretched out.

Slowly the idol sloshed forward toward Ashtir, driven by the berserk spirit of The Thief-Taker.

Slowly the two giants met in ghastly embrace.

Jaal's brazen arms slipped around the woman also carved

of bronze. Brak's perch became treacherous. Harder the Jaal-thing embraced the bronze woman, *harder*—

Ashtir began to crack apart. Below, in the hollow center of the statue's body, light flooded in. Brak was nearly blinded by the blaze of ghostly fire from the cyclopean eye of Jaal just in front of him.

Slowly, locked in the embrace, the two idols began to tip toward the water.

Brak had a fleeting impression of Ilona stretching out her hand to him. Her face was old, her hair no longer yellow but white, her voice cried over the noise:

"Barbarian— —I acknowledge—defeat. Stretch out your hand—save me from—"

A segment of collapsing bronze from the Ashtir statue's neck struck Ilona, smashed her against Jaal's bronze shoulder, stifling her scream, crushing her in a ghastly eruption of pulp and blood.

The whole world whirled around the big barbarian as the Ashtir statue cracked apart.

He fell through space, turning over and over, now toward the blazing sun, now toward the cobalt water. With a roar to shake the universe, both statues struck the sea, still locked together.

Brak hit a moment later.

He came shooting to the surface, retching and spitting. Far away, armor gleamed on the mole.

With a last effort of his tortured body, Brak the barbarian hauled himself along in the water. Behind him, eruptions and explosions burst through the harbor's surface. A great chain of bubbles streamed up from beneath the sea, popped open, exuding a death-smell that was blown to nothing on the wind.

Presently the sea was quiet except for a few small bubbles that signified the last settling of the idols in their grisly embrace at the bottom of the harbor.

Brak the barbarian struck his skull against the crumbled mole. He felt the stout hands of armored soldiers lift him from the water, pluck clumsily at the Lamb Fleece still knotted around his shoulder. He tried to speak:

"Here, here is the Fleece which—"

He knew nothing more.

So it was that the people of Rodar's city-state, the Kingdom of the Two Bays, regained their holy emblem.

Soldiers rushed it to the central square, together with tidings that the idols had sunk beneath the water. At this news, the citizens rallied. They took to the rooftops and, after a battle which raged on through the night and all the next day, they hurled the invaders from the city, using weapons no more lethal than stones and arrows. But these weapons, discharged from roofs where the scythe-chariots were useless, won the day.

That second night also, trumpets blew on the plain. The disbelieving people saw the Gord retreat turn into total disaster as Prince Rodar appeared, not dead at all as the rumor had said, but only forced into hiding after his army's defeat at the frontier. The Prince had re-gathered scattered bands of soldiers and arrived at the city in time to catch the retreating Gord forces from the rear. On a field of blood he obliterated them, and their threat to harm his kingdom ever again. Caught between the pincers of army and populace, every last Gord warrior died. And, it was said, in their far-off capital, the women, the graybeards and the children—the only ones left behind—went into perpetual mourning and smashed the idols of the goat-god in their temples.

But these tidings Brak the barbarian did not learn for many days, until he wakened again—this time under more auspicious circumstances—in the household of Phonicios.

Once more it was Saria who tended him. Her own light arrow-wound was on the way to healing. After a suitable period of rest, Brak grew impatient to be up and about.

Thus it happened that, one misty pink dawn, after Brak had been feted at court by Prince Rodar for several days and nights, a small group of people assembled in the courtyard of Phonicios's house.

At the rear of the group, several servants were making coarse jokes about the vizier, Mustaf ben Medi, who had been banished for his bumbling. Phonicios shushed them with a stern look.

"This is a splendid pony, lord," Brak commented. He eyed the beast who stamped impatiently. "Far better than an outlander deserves."

Phonicios clapped the big barbarian's shoulder warmly. His face had filled out. He once more wore the robes of the chief of the Merchant Guild, the position having been restored to him by unanimous vote of his fellow-members.

"It's but a tiny particle of what you deserve, Brak," Phonicios said. "Except for you, this city would not stand here today."

Brak swung up on the pony's back. Saria stood close beside Calix. The freedman had his arm around her waist. Both bade Brak a warm farewell.

Phonicios grasped Brak's saddle-thong. "Why don't you stay? There is a place for you in my household, Brak. I'll promise you tasks worthy of your powers, and a respected position in the hierarchy of Rodar's city. The Prince himself said as much at court when he thanked you for what you had done for his kingdom."

Smiling sadly, Brak shook his head. "A tempting offer, lord. Were I to take it—" His shrug was simple, yet eloquent. "I would not be the man I am, born to wander the world until I find whatever it is that's waiting for me in Khurdisan."

He lifted his hand. The watchers in the lonely courtyard shielded their eyes against the misty pink sunrise until pony and man were lost among the maze of streets.